MW01235261

Murder in the Bowling Alley

Other books written by the author:

Make For a Better Place
God's Twin Earth
Retribution

Murder in the Bowling Alley

Robert M. Beatty

Copyright © 2017 by Robert M. Beatty.

Library of Congress Control Number: 2017904819
ISBN: Hardcover   978-1-5434-1192-8
               Softcover   978-1-5434-1191-1
               eBook   978-1-5434-1190-4

All rights reserved. No part of this book may be reproduced or transmitted in any form or by any means, electronic or mechanical, including photocopying, recording, or by any information storage and retrieval system, without permission in writing from the copyright owner.

Murder in the Bowling Alley is a work of fiction. Names, characters, locals, and incidents are used fictitiously. Any resemblance to persons living or dead, events, or businesses is entirely coincidental.

Any people depicted in stock imagery provided by Thinkstock are models, and such images are being used for illustrative purposes only.
Certain stock imagery © Thinkstock.

Print information available on the last page.

Rev. date: 03/28/2017

To order additional copies of this book, contact:
Xlibris
1-888-795-4274
www.Xlibris.com
Orders@Xlibris.com
758908

A special thank you to my son, Randy Beatty, and my wife, Cleo, for her assistance. Also, special thanks to Scott Cox, my computer consultant, and to the staff at Xlibris, without whose help this book would never have been printed.

CHAPTER ONE

Twenty-six years ago, the Stay Healthy and Have Fun club decided to organize a bowling league. Since there were sixteen members who wanted to bowl, four teams were set up consisting of four members each. They met at one o'clock each Wednesday afternoon at Piedmont Bowling. The original rules under which the bowlers participated have remained the same from the first day that the first ball was rolled down the lane. The league has, however, grown from the original four teams to fourteen teams of four members each.

Although the bowlers in the Seniors' Bowling League enjoyed winning, they enjoyed socializing just as much, or maybe even more. They socialized before the bowling game started, continued throughout the competition, and continued still for several minutes after the competition was over. A number of members got together during the week to attend various functions.

In the time that the league has been in existence, there has never been a dispute of any kind until three weeks earlier, when a man who gave his name as Ben

Zinch walked into Piedmont Bowling and said he would like to bowl. Since the second place team, who called themselves the Owls, had just lost a member due to an accident, he was invited to bowl with them.

About halfway through the second game, Zinch left the five pin standing after rolling his first ball. As soon as his ball was returned, he took aim and rolled his second ball toward the standing pin. It missed. As soon as the ball passed the pin without hitting it, he let loose with a string of obscenities. Before he could sit down, Jesse Moore, the owner-manager, was in his face.

"I don't know where you're used to bowling," Jesse said, looking Zinch straight in his eyes, "but that kind of language is not permitted here. This is a family-oriented business, and even if it wasn't, your fellow bowlers do not want to hear it. Is that clear?"

At first Zinch only glared at Jesse and said nothing. Then when Jesse did not say anything either but kept staring at him, Zinch said in a belligerent tone, "Yeah, I heard you."

"Then I expect you to follow our rules. If you do, we'll forget about this."

Zinch mumbled, "OK," and Jesse walked away.

The next bowling date was on the first Wednesday of the month. On this day, certain members of the league brought in cakes to celebrate the birthdays of each bowler whose birthday was in that month. The members referred to it as Cake Day.

When Zinch came in, he sat at the edge of the group without saying a word. When he was offered a piece of cake, he gave a quick retort. "I don't eat stuff like that." The person offering the cake turned and walked away, and Zinch continued to sit alone until the bowling game started.

The next week, the Owls, who were still in second place, bowled the Hawks, the first-place team *for position*. The Hawks won the first game, and the Owls won the second game. The third game was down to the wire. The Owls had finished bowling, but Carl Simmons, the anchor for the Hawks, had not yet bowled. The scores were so close that if Simmons made either a strike or a spare and then hit at least two pins, the Hawks would win.

Simmons stepped up to the line, stood there a few seconds, and then rolled the ball. It looked like a perfect hit, but when the pins were through flopping around, the ten pin was left standing. As soon as his ball was returned, he picked it up and took his place on the line. He aimed carefully and rolled the ball. At first the pin just wobbled, and then it fell.

Zinch immediately jumped up, claiming the ball had gone into the gutter but came out before it hit the ten pin, so he didn't make a spare. Members of both teams looked at Zinch like they could not believe what he just said. One of his own team members said, "Ben, that ball didn't go near the gutter," as Simmons picked up his ball and prepared to roll it again.

Zinch immediately jumped to his feet, his face flushed and his fists clenched. He got in front of Simmons so he could not roll the ball and started spewing obscenities in his face.

Before Zinch finished, Jesse Moore jumped between them. He yelled two words, *"Get out!"*

"You son of a bitch, this is a public place. You can't throw me out!" Zinch yelled back.

"I can and I just did," Jesse replied in a more quiet tone, forcing himself to regain his composure. "Now get your ball and get out of here before I call the cops and have you arrested for trespassing."

"Then I'll give them something to arrest me for!" Zinch shouted as he started to take swing at him.

Before the punch landed, his arm was grabbed by Tim Harper, a six-foot-three, two hundred and ten-pound bowler who had been standing by, watching the confrontation. He very quietly said, "I believe you were told to leave."

Zinch spun around, ready to fight whoever it was who had grabbed his arm. When he saw Tim Harper, even as mad and out of control as he was, he decided that would not be a good idea. Instead, he turned and walked over to the ball return rack, grabbed his ball, put into the bag, and walked out the door.

As soon as Zinch was out the door, Jesse turned to Carl Simmons and said, "I believe you can bowl now."

Simmons, who knew everybody in the building was watching him, took his place at the line. He knew he had to hit two or more pins to win, but the pressure got to him. He rolled the ball and hit only one pin, ending the game in a tie.

CHAPTER TWO

Ben Zinch was irate. He swore to himself that he would get even with the man who had thrown him out of the bowling alley, overlooking the fact he had caused his own removal. He was so mad he did not even notice it was softly raining.

When Zinch got to his car, he opened the trunk and slammed the bag containing his bowling ball and shoes into the trunk so hard that they bounced off the back of the trunk. Then he opened the car door and jumped into the driver's seat.

As soon as he was seated, Zinch put the key into the ignition, but before he could start the engine, there was a knock on the window beside him. He looked through the glass. A man wearing a raincoat and a rain hat he had never seen before was standing there, signaling him to roll down the window. Without thinking, he rolled it down to see what the man wanted. He had not seen the man follow him out of the building alley and had not seen him approach the car. Without introducing himself, the man said, "I saw what happened in there, and that guy had no business throwing you out. It's a damn shame when a man can't express himself without being told to leave the building."

"Yeah, but what the hell do you care? Who are you anyway?"

"Just call me Sam. I thought you might be interested in getting even with him. If you let me in the car, we can talk about it."

Without waiting for an answer, Sam walked to the other side of the car. As soon as he was beside the door, Zinch unlocked it, and he slipped in beside him.

Zinch took a long look at the man who had just entered his car. He had never seen him before and wondered why he had let him. "I don't know you, and I don't know what the hell you want. What are you talking about, getting a chance to get even? Why is this any business of yours to start with? So either start talking or get out."

"Let's just say that I have a reason for wanting to get even with that bastard in there. I'm familiar with this building, and I can disable that poor excuse they have for an alarm. I know where they keep their money, and I can get into the safe to get it."

By now, Zinch had calmed down a little and was beginning to realize what this man was telling him. "Why are you telling all of this to me? If you can do everything you claim you can do, why do you need me? How do you know I won't go to the police?"

"What are you going to tell them? That some guy you don't know is going to do something to the guy that manages the bowling alley? I don't think so," Sam answered. "But to answer your questions, it's because I saw what happened to you, and I thought you might like to get even and maybe pick up a little money while you're doing it. I don't give a damn about the money. You can have it all. I just want to make as much trouble for that bastard as I can, and I thought you might want to help me do it. Revenge makes a body feel good."

Zinch started to think. Maybe he could team up with this guy and then leave town as soon as the job was done. Nobody knew him there. He really wanted to *put that guy in his place.*

"I don't know about this. I want to get even with that bastard, but this sounds pretty risky. It seems to me like we stand a good chance of getting caught."

Sam answered, "Well, to start with, we won't get caught. We will go in through a hole in the back wall. Then I'll disable the alarm. We'll get the job done and then leave through the same hole."

Zinch did not understand what Sam was talking about. "What do you mean, 'a hole in the wall'? You talking about a back door?"

"You'll see when we get back there," Sam assured him. "Don't worry about it."

Zinch thought about it some more. He really did not want to do this, but he sure wanted to give that manager as much trouble as he could. But he was afraid the cops would immediately suspect him because of what had transpired. He thought some more. Suddenly, he thought of a way to get an alibi. He just had to make sure he was not fingerprinted.

"If I agree to do this, we will have to do it after midnight. I want my wife to be able to swear I went to bed with her and I did not get up until morning. She's a sound sleeper, and I'm pretty sure I can slip out for an hour or so after she goes to sleep and not be missed." He was so angry and so intent on punishing the bowling alley manager that he did not think about how weak this would be as an alibi. He had convinced himself that he could get away with it. If necessary, he could disappear.

"Okay, buddy," Sam said. "If you tell me where you live, I'll pick you up at midnight. Don't let me down now."

"No. You will not pick me up. I don't want you to know where I live. There's an all-night restaurant in the next block up from here, and no one will pay any attention to cars parked in their lot. I'll see you there at fifteen minutes after twelve."

Sam got out of the car. Without saying another word, he closed the door behind him.

At the appointed time, Sam and Zinch met in the parking lot as planned, and then walked together down the street to the back of the bowling alley. Instead of there being a door, there was what appeared to be a sheet of metal bolted to the back of the building. Sam reached into his pants pocket and took out something that looked like some kind of electronic device. He handed it to Zinch and told him to hold it.

"What's that?" Zinch asked.

"That's a little gadget I invented. It will tell me if there is an alarm system, and if there is, it will give me the code needed to disarm it. It's the only one in the entire country," he bragged.

Zinch questioned that claim in his mind but said nothing as he watched Sam take out a wrench and remove the bolts. After the bolts were taken out and the sheet metal removed, Zinch saw a hole in the wall where a door had been. The door was completely gone, and the wood in the framing around the door was splintered. Some of the bricks that had been around the door were also missing.

"Wait a minute," Sam said as he grabbed Zinch to keep him from going into the building. "My detector shows there's an alarm near the opening." As Zinch stepped back, Sam entered the hole. A few seconds later, he came back out. "Now it's safe to come in."

When they were inside the building, they walked through the door leading to the bowling area. After they had taken a few steps, Sam took an old .38-caliber revolver from his other pants pocket.

"What's that for?" Zinch said, looking at the gun. "What you have the gun for?"

"To kill you with," Sam answered, as he pointed the gun directly at Zinch.

"What the hell are you doing? I knew I shouldn't have trust you. You bastard!" Zinch yelled. "Are you crazy?"

"No, I'm not crazy. Now you stand there, or sit down if you prefer, but keep your hands where I can see them. I'm going to tell you a story."

Zinch remained standing. He realized Sam was serious, and he wanted to be able to move in a hurry if he saw a chance to grab the gun from him.

Sam continued. "About nineteen or twenty years ago, while I was in the joint for killing a guy, my brother was dating Jesse Moore's daughter. That's the name of the guy who threw you out, in case you didn't know it. She was fourteen, but she told my brother she was sixteen. He was nineteen. One night, when her parents were out of town, they went to the movies. When my brother took her home, she led him into her bedroom, where they had sex for the first time. They did the same thing the next night, but while they were having sex, her parents come home, and when her father opened her bedroom door, she screamed.

"Jesse Moore called the police, and my brother was arrested before he left the house. He tried to convince Moore the sex was consensual, but Moore would not believe his *little girl* would do anything like that. He insisted she testify against my brother, and he was convicted and given a prison sentence. The second night he was in prison, he killed himself."

Zinch was now desperate. He was certain Sam was going to kill him, but he could not figure where he fit into the picture. He considered screaming, but he knew if he did Sam would shoot.

"What do you have to kill me for? Put that gun away, and I'll help you kill Moore. You know you will be caught and sent back to prison."

"No, I won't be caught. My second wife left me a bunch of money. My last wife left me even more, so I deal only in cash and leave no paper trail. I don't want to kill Jesse Moore. I want him to suffer for the rest of his life. And that daughter of his, I got a little something in mind for her too. Oh, I forgot. When they find your body, they will find a note in your pocket from Jesse Moore asking you to come down to the bowling alley about ten o'clock so he can make it up to you for the way he treated you."

Zinch was now terrified. He knew he had to act now. He jumped to one side and lunged for the gun, but Sam was prepared for him. He brought him down with one shot to his heart.

Since he had stolen the gun some time ago in Walla Walla, Washington, Sam threw it beside Zinch's body. "You should have picked out a better partner in crime," he said as he walked around Zinch's body on his way to the bowling alley office. When he got into the office, he scattered all the papers he could find in their file cabinets over the floor. He made no attempt to open the safe but did find an envelope holding some money on top of one of the cabinets which he took.

When he walked back through the hole they had come in through, Sam looked down at the wrench and said, "You'll be needed to put the plate back on." He continued walking until he got to where his car was parked.

He put the key into the ignition and started the engine. He was hungry, but he knew better than to be seen in the restaurant. As he drove away, he said aloud, "As I told Zinch, revenge will be sweet." Then he drove to the house he had rented two months before. Since the owner lived in Michigan, she would probably not even hear about any of this, he thought to himself. And if she did, she would not think about that nice young man who had a wife and two little girls who rented her house online.

CHAPTER THREE

Jesse Moore had not slept well. As soon as he went to bed, he started thinking about the incident at the bowling alley earlier that day and became wide awake. He tossed and turned for an hour before finally giving up.

After Jesse got up from his bed, he walked over to his lounge chair and picked up a novel he had started several days before. Usually if he could not sleep, he could get out of bed and read until the words made no sense, and then he could return to bed and sleep would take over.

Tonight was different. Even as he was reading, he could not get the incident off his mind. He knew he had done the right thing by ordering Ben Zinch to leave the bowling alley, but he was furious with himself for having lost his composure and shouting back at Zinch. Finally, after reading for over an hour, the words failed to have any meaning, so he returned to his bed.

After he returned to bed, he went to sleep, but at 4:30 a.m., he awakened. The first thing that entered his mind was the incident, and he could not shake it off. He got out of bed, shaved, and took a shower. Then he made himself a cup of coffee from his single-cup coffeemaker.

When Jesse was about half through with his coffee, he heard his newspaper slam against the front door. He retrieved it from the porch, and for a short period, the articles in the paper interested him, but after a few minutes, he started thinking about the incident at the bowling alley again. He wondered if there could be any repercussions. Could he be in violation of any of the civil rights laws? Could he be sued? All these questions kept whirling around in his head until he heard a knock on his front door. While he was walking toward the door to see who was there, he glanced at his watch and was surprised to see that it was only seven o'clock. He thought he had been awake much longer than that.

When he opened the door, he was greeted by his partner, Roy Arnold, and Jeff Sadler, their attorney. He assumed one of the employees who worked the counter had called Roy, and he called Sadler.

"Come in," Jesse said, stepping back from the door. "You guys are getting an early start. Evidently you heard about our little incident yesterday, and now you want all the details."

"Good morning, Jesse," Roy responded. "Yeah, we heard you had a little problem. Why don't we go get some breakfast and talk about it?"

"Sounds good to me," Jesse said. "Earl McNeill is going to open up this morning, so we don't have to be in any hurry to get through eating."

All three walked out to Roy's car, got in, buckled up, and drove to the nearby neighborhood restaurant. As soon as they arrived, they walked in, grabbed a booth, and ordered coffee. After they finished drinking their first cup, they ordered another cup to drink with their breakfast.

"Okay, Jesse," Roy said. "Let's have it. What happened?"

Jesse went into great detail, starting with the first day that Ben Zinch walked in and said he would like to bowl on a team. He told them how he had to chastise him the first time he bowled for the language he used after missing a pin. Then he gave the details leading to the incident in question before asking, "Do we have a legal problem?"

Roy turned to Sadler, their attorney. "Do we have a problem?"

Sadler, who was caught with his mouth full of food, said, after swallowing, "I don't see any."

"See, Jesse, no problem."

"That's good," he answered. "You guys know that I have managed that bowling alley for about thirty years without having any problems. That senior league is composed of the nicest people you can find anywhere. Then some bastard comes along and screws up my record."

Roy looked at Jesse. "Jesse, you've done a great job. No one is blaming you. Something like this was bound to happen sometime. Shake it off. Don't let it bother you."

Just then, Jesse's cell phone rang.

"Jesse, get over here as soon as you can!" Earl McNeill shouted into the phone and then hung up without furnishing any information or waiting for an answer.

CHAPTER FOUR

Jesse Moore, along with Roy Arnold and Jeff Sadler, rushed out of the restaurant and jumped into Roy's car. Driving faster than he had ever driven within the city and zigzagging in and out of traffic, he got them to the bowling alley in record time. There were three police cars in the parking lot with their lights flashing. Another one drove in behind them.

Without making any effort to contact those officers, they leaped from the car and rushed to the front door. It was blocked by a uniformed police officer Jesse knew.

"What's going on, Jim?" Jesse shouted as they rushed up to the door. "Why are all the police here?"

"You better get in there, Jesse. They're waiting for you," Jim answered without furnishing any information. They rushed in and went straight to the counter, where two uniformed police officers and three other people were standing. Earl McNeill was standing behind the counter.

When Jesse reached the group, he looked across the floor. He saw what looked like a man crumpled on the bowling lane by the wall. He looked like Ben Zinch, but he was not sure. "Is that Ben Zinch?" he asked Earl McNeill.

"Yes it is," he answered in almost a whisper.

Now Jesse was completely befuddled, but before he could say or do anything, the only woman in the group walked over to him.

"I'm Helen Martin, chief detective of the Piedmont Police Department, Mr. Moore. Why don't we walk over to one of the bowler's tables where we can talk about this," she said as she took hold of his arm and led him toward the table. When they were seated, she glanced at Jesse, who looked as though he would pass out any second.

"Apparently, you know the man lying on the floor over there," she said softly.

Jesse was still in a daze. He jumped when she spoke to him, like he was hearing her for the first time. "What? What did you say? Mrs.—" He could not remember her name.

"I'm Helen Martin. I'm a detective," she told him again. "We are trying to find out what has happened here, and I need you to help me. Will you do that?"

Jesse struggled to regain his composure. "I'll try, Mrs. Martin. What did you ask me?"

"I know what you are going through, Mr. Moore. I really do. Why don't you call me Helen, and I'll call you Jesse. Maybe that will make you more comfortable." While she was talking, Helen took out a small recording device and placed it on the table. "Do you mind if I record our conversation? It saves me from having to take notes, and I can concentrate more on our discussion."

"No, I don't mind," Jesse responded, "but tell me what's going on. How did Ben Zinch get in here? Why is he here? Was he shot? If he was, who shot him?"

"Give me a minute, Jesse, and I'll tell you everything I know," she said. Then she continued without waiting for him to reply. "At around eight thirty this morning, we got a call from your employee, Earl McNeill, who said he had just opened up the bowling alley and there was a dead man in there. As soon as he hung up, Ken Matthews, John Patton, and I rushed over here as quickly as we could. When we got here, I verified that the man he said was Ben Zinch was dead. Then I called for uniformed officers to block off the area and keep everybody out and had Earl McNeill call you. I didn't know you were going to show up with two other men I don't know, but I assume they have some business here. Ken and John will talk to them."

Jess interrupted her. "Roy Arnold is my partner. He has nothing to do with the operation of the bowling alley.

His only interest is financial. Jeff Sadler is an attorney we use for our business. He does not have anything to do with the operation of the bowling alley either."

Detective Martin continued. "Your employee said the deceased is a man who bowled here yesterday by the name of Ben Zinch. He said you threw him out of the bowling alley yesterday because of the obscene language he was using."

"Yes, I did," Jesse admitted, and then he continued. "But I haven't seen him since then. I don't understand. Why is he here? How did he get in? What happened to him?"

Helen waited patiently, and then she put her hand on his shoulder. "That's what we have to find out, Jesse."

Jesse turned to face her. "I'm sorry, Helen, but I'm so confused."

"I understand, Jesse. Can I get you anything? Water? Cola?"

"No, thanks. I'm all right now. Please go ahead."

Helen continued. "After I verified that the man was deceased, I called for the crime scene investigators. They should be here shortly." She paused briefly, waiting for Jesse to comment. When he did not say anything, she said, "Tell me everything that led to your asking Zinch to leave the bowling alley, Jesse."

Jesse thought for a minute, and then he told her about how Zinch came into the bowling alley and asked to bowl on a team, how he cautioned him about his language the first time he bowled, and how that led to his being asked to leave. He ended by telling her he had not seen him since then, until he saw him lying crumpled on the floor just then.

Just as Jesse finished talking, Lou Barns, captain of the Piedmont Police Department who was in charge of the crime scene investigation, motioned Helen over to where he was standing. When she joined him, he told her that Zinch's entrance into the building apparently was through a large hole in the back wall of the building that had been covered by two four-by-eight pieces of metal. He said there had been a door under the metal which had been plintered a long time ago, judging by the appearance of it. He said he had no other information since they were just getting started on their search.

Helen thanked him and returned to the table, where Jesse was still sitting. "Now, Jesse, can you think of any possible reason why Ben Zinch would have come over to the bowling alley after you had closed?"

"No," Jesse said almost in a whisper. "I can't."

"Can you think of any way Zinch could have gotten into the building without setting off the alarms?"

"I just don't know," Jesse answered while holding his head in his hands.

"How about that big hole in the wall that had been covered with steel plates bolted to the wall?"

"Did he take the plates off?"

"Yes, he did. Tell me about that hole, Jesse."

"That happened before I bought the bowling alley. I was told that a truck backed into the building and splintered the door and knocked some of the bricks off. The truck was not insured, and the driver didn't have the money to fix the damage. Neither did the bowling alley owner, but they located two steel plates and had them bolted to the wall. They have been there ever since. I just can't believe it. How did he get past the motion detector that picks up any movement within about ten feet from the door?"

"I don't know, Jesse, but we are going to find out before we get through," she assured him. "Can you get a complete list of the people who bowled yesterday?"

"Yes, we can get that information for you. Loretta Jefferson is the president of the league, and she will probably have more telephone numbers than we have. If there is a bowler whose telephone number she doesn't have, someone on that team will probably have it. Do you want me to call her and have her come in?"

"Yes, I do," Helen replied. "Why don't you stay where you are, and I'll have McNeill call her?"

As Helen approached the counter, she met the other detectives.

"What did you get out of the guy you talked to?" she asked Ken Matthews.

"I talked to Roy Arnold," he answered. "He has no part in the operation of the bowling alley. He put up the money so Jesse Moore could buy the place, and Moore is making monthly payments to repay him. I let him go, but I told him to stick around in case we needed to talk to him again."

"What about Jeff Sadler, John?"

"He's an attorney who does legal work for Jesse Moore once in a while. He has nothing to do with the operation of the bowling alley either. I let him go too."

"Have the officers doing the neighborhood investigation come in yet?"

Just then, Earl McNeill signaled to Helen. "Loretta Jefferson will be in within thirty minutes," he told her.

"Great. I'll tell whoever is on the door to let her in," she said as she walked toward the door.

Chapter Five

Thirty minutes after she received the telephone call, Loretta Jefferson pulled into the bowling alley parking lot. All she had been told during the telephone call was that she was urgently needed. When she saw all the police cars with their lights flashing, her imagination ran wild. She imagined many things that could have happened but never once thought of someone being murdered, their body left in the bowling alley.

She was so nervous, she just sat still in her car for a few seconds. When she did get out, she almost slammed the car door with the keys left in the ignition. She caught it just before it hit the latch. After she stopped the door from shutting, she just stood there telling herself to calm down and go inside where she was needed.

The silent lecture she gave herself worked. She reached into the car, removed the key from the ignition, and gently shut the door. Then she quickly walked to the front door of the bowling alley. She identified herself to the officer on duty who opened the door and let her enter. She headed toward the counter, but as she approached it, she looked across the bowling lanes. As she did, she noticed what seemed to be a man lying on the last bowling lane nearest the wall. Somehow, she just knew he was dead. She thought she was going to lose her breakfast, but with a great deal of effort, she pulled herself together.

"I'm Helen Martin, chief of detectives, Piedmont Police Department," Helen said as she introduced herself to Loretta. "I'm sorry we have to meet under these conditions, Ms. Jefferson, but we need to get started on this investigation as soon as possible, and I did not want to wait until the crime scene investigators have approved the renewal of the victim's body."

Loretta just stared at Helen without saying anything.

Helen took hold of Loretta's arm. "Let's walk over to the table where Jesse Moore is sitting," she said to her as she started walking toward the table with her.

When they reached the table, Loretta, without greeting Jesse, said, "Is that Ben Zinch over there on the floor?"

"Yes, it is," Jesse told her without looking up.

"I don't understand. What's going on? Why is he here? How did he get in? What killed him?"

Before Loretta could continue, Helen interrupted her. "Earl McNeill just made a new pot of coffee, Loretta. Would you like a cup?"

"Yes, please. Maybe a cup of black coffee will calm my stomach down."

"I think I would like another cup myself," Helen said as she signaled to McNeill by holding up two fingers.

"Have a seat, Ms. Jefferson—"

"Please call me Loretta," she said. "Should I call you Detective?"

"Detective or Helen, whichever you prefer," Helen answered. Then she started to say something, but when she noticed McNeill coming toward them with two cups of coffee, she waited until he set them on the table.

"I hope you like your coffee black," McNeill said before asking, "Would you like a cup of coffee, Mr. Moore?"

"No, thanks," Jesse replied.

"Okay, Loretta, let's get started," Helen said after they had drained their coffee cups. "Do you know Ben Zinch?"

"I met him the first day he started bowling in the league. I saw him each time he bowled after that, but I never talked to him on those days," Loretta said. "I saw and heard Jesse order him out of the bowling alley following his tirade."

"Do you know if anybody who was bowling yesterday knew him before he started bowling with your league? Or did you ever see anyone come in with him?"

"No. He seemed to stay by himself, except when he was sitting at the table waiting his turn to bowl."

"Do you have any idea how he got into the bowling alley, or why he was in the building last night?"

"No, I don't."

"Did he ever mention a wife or any other relative?"

"Not that I ever heard. He may have said something to the bowlers on his team."

"Do you have his telephone number?"

Just then, Jesse interrupted them. "I need to use the restroom, Helen. The men's room is over by the wall where Ben Zinch is."

"Use the ladies' restroom since it's on this side of the building, Jesse. I don't want you walking through the crime scene."

Helen continued. "Loretta, that's all the questions I have for now, but we may have to interview everybody who bowled yesterday. Jesse said they could give us a printout showing the names of the bowler but that you would have more telephone numbers than they do. Also, what do you think their attitude would be if you called them and asked them to come to the police station?"

Loretta answered quickly, "These people are going to want to do everything they can to get whoever killed Ben Zinch caught. Most of them know little or nothing about him, but he may have told his teammates something about his background. I have a telephone number for most of the bowlers that were here yesterday. If you want me to, I can go with you to the police department, make my calls from there, and check them off as they come in."

"That sounds like a perfect plan, Loretta. Wait here until I check with the crime scene investigators and the officers who were doing a neighborhood check."

Loretta watched as Helen walked over to where the officers were working on the other side of the bowling alley. They exchanged only a few words, and then she turned and walked back toward her.

When Helen got back to where Loretta was sitting, the front door opened, and a uniformed officer came in and walked over to her.

"Do us any good, Hank?"

"Nothing, Helen," he answered. "The bowling alley is surrounded by small businesses, and we talked to someone at every shop with the exception of two who had not opened yet. I left one of the officers standing by to talk to them when they get in. Sorry I couldn't do you any good."

"Thanks, Hank. That's about what I expected. Let your guys go back to their regular work. Before you release them though, see if the name Ben Zinch means anything to them. We think that's the murdered guy's name. He was ordered out of the bowling alley about three or three thirty yesterday afternoon, and so far, I haven't found anyone who has seen him since then until now."

"I'll put the word out, Helen. You know we'll help if we can." He turned and walked away.

As Hank turned to leave, Helen motioned for the other two detectives to join her at the table. When they got there, she asked, "Is there any more you can do here?"

Both detectives agreed they had done all they could at the bowling alley.

"Okay then," Helen said. "Check all the sources and see if you can find out anything about this guy. So far, we have nothing. When you get that done, come on in to the station, and we'll have a meeting at two thirty."

They turned to leave.

"One other thing," she said. "It looks like we may have to interview everyone who was here yesterday when Zinch was told to leave. Loretta will come in with me to my office and start calling the bowlers from there. As they come in, we will interview each one until the last one has gone home. It's going to be a long afternoon, so why don't we all get a bite to eat and then get busy?"

Both Ken and John agreed. "We'll see you there," they said.

"If you would like to join me for lunch, Loretta, I would love to have you, and then you can follow me over to the police department."

"That's fine with me," Loretta answered.

CHAPTER SIX

When Helen Martin and Loretta Jefferson arrived at the police department, Helen drove into the police officers' parking area, and Loretta parked her car in the visitors' parking area. After getting out of their cars, they walked together into Helen's office.

Ken Matthews and John Patton were inside her office waiting for them. As soon as Helen saw them, she asked, "Did you get anything?"

Ken answered, "We found no record of anyone by the name of Ben Zinch anywhere. We checked with the light company, gas company, telephone company, and none of them had anyone listed by that name. No driver's license or auto registration in that name either."

Helen motioned for Loretta to have a seat at her desk so she could use her telephone to make the calls to the bowlers. Then she checked her incoming calls. She had three. The first two were about two other cases she was working on. The last call was from Captain Barns. She let the recorder play so they could all hear what he had to say. He sure got their attention with his message:

"Sorry I'm late, Helen, but I've gotten a good bit of information. First of all, our victim's name is not Zinch, it's Benjamin Barlow. There's warrants outstanding. The last one is because he and another man robbed a bank in Springfield, Illinois. I'll be over there in about ten minutes and will fill you in when I get there."

No sooner had the recorder quit playing when Captain Barns walked into Helen's office. Before he had a chance to say anything, Helen said, "Let's go down to one of the interview rooms so Loretta can make her calls while the captain fills us in."

As the others started to leave, Helen said, "Loretta, you heard what Captain Barns said about Zinch's name actually being Barlow. Don't give that information to his teammates you are going to call. Oh, call Bob Johns at the bowling alley too. He worked yesterday, and he wasn't in when we were there this morning. As soon as the first one gets here, walk down the hall and knock on the door marked 'interview room number one.' I'll tell the duty officer our plans."

After giving Loretta her instructions, Helen walked to the interview room to join the others. As soon as she arrived, she walked over and sat on the desk rather than walking around and sitting on the chair behind it. "Okay, Lou, bring us up to date."

Lou commenced giving his report. "As soon as I got the results of the fingerprint check from the FBI, I called the Springfield Police Department and talked to the duty officer. It seems that about ten years ago, Benjamin Barlow and a Lou Hardy robbed a bank which was located in Springfield. They apparently got a lot of money, and on the way out of the bank, before they got to their getaway car, Barlow shot Hardy in the leg, threw the money into the car, and drove away, leaving Hardy lying on the ground. The money has never been recovered.

"I called the prison where Hardy is incarcerated and talked to him briefly. He immediately admitted knowing Barlow, and when I told him Barlow is dead, he said, and I am quoting, 'I'm glad that son of a bitch is dead. Now I won't have to kill him when get out.' He said he didn't know any of his relatives, but he hesitated a little before answering that question."

"Man, you've been busy, Lou. Did you get any indication that Hardy may have set up this killing? I don't think we can overlook this possibility, although we have no way of knowing right now."

"No, I didn't, Helen. Like I said, I only talked to him for a few minutes, and he has had ten years to hate this guy. We probably need to know if anyone that has been released in the last few months was especially friendly with Hardy."

Just then, there was a knock on the door, and after a "Come in," Loretta opened the door.

"One of the dead man's teammates is in your office, Helen. The first thing he said to me after I told him what this is all about was 'Did that guy who followed him out the door do it?' That's the first I've heard about the other man, and I don't know if you've heard about him or not."

"Thanks, Loretta, I'll be there in a couple of minutes. If any of the others get there before I do, send them down here, but keep him in my office."

"Yes, ma'am," she answered as she closed the door behind her.

"Did any of you hear about anyone following the victim out of the building?" she asked. They each replied they had not heard this before.

"I think this new information forces us to interview each bowler that was there yesterday. I think we have to do it this evening. I certainly don't have to tell you guys how to conduct an interview. Let's work through the list as quickly as we can. We can always have them return if you have a reason to do so. Remember to not mention the gun," Helen said before she walked out the door to return to her office.

As soon as Helen walked into her office, she introduced herself to the bowler sitting there waiting for her. Before she started to interview him, she instructed Loretta to go to interview room number two and start calling all the other bowlers.

CHAPTER SEVEN

Helen Martin's alarm clock awakened her from a sound sleep at 5:45 a.m. She really did not want to get up from her bed. Her body told her it needed to stay there for at least another hour or two to make up for her having stayed up so late the night before. She was still tired. They had not finished interviewing the bowlers until after ten o'clock, and by the time she finished eating a cheeseburger and reviewing her notes and finally got into bed, it was past midnight.

She gave in and allowed herself the luxury of hitting the snooze button on her alarm clock once before making herself get up. She thoroughly enjoyed those extra ten minutes of bedtime. She considered skipping her stretching exercises, but then her better judgment took over, and she did them as she did every morning. When she was finished with the exercises, she grabbed a shower, put on her face, and fixed her hair before slipping into a light navy blue business suit.

After she readied herself for the work that lay ahead of her, she walked to her car and started driving toward a café near the police department. As she was on her way, she started mentally reviewing yesterday's activities: first, a man who had introduced himself as Ben Zinch was found dead in Piedmont Bowling from a gunshot wound. Then after sending his fingerprints to the FBI, they learned his true name was Benjamin Barlow. When she was interviewing bowlers who had bowled with Barlow, whom they knew as Ben Zinch, two reported seeing an unknown man following Barlow out of the bowling alley. They could only describe him as a white man who was wearing a raincoat and a rain hat. They estimated his height to be between five feet ten inches and six feet. They did not know the identity of any of the victim's friends or relatives. The other bowlers she interviewed furnished no information of value.

After Helen got through tossing that information around in her head, she estimated that by the time she got to the café, she would just have enough time to get some breakfast and get to her office for the scheduled meeting at eight o'clock.

When she arrived at the café and was pulling into the parking lot, Helen saw Ken Matthews and John Patton pulling in behind her. They all got out of their cars and walked into the café together. They headed toward an empty booth. As soon as the waitress saw them, she set three cups of black coffee on the table without waiting for them to order. They placed their breakfast order, and while they were eating, they kept the conversation light. They had established a rule a few months earlier that they would not discuss their cases while eating. When they finished their breakfast, they proceeded to their cars and drove to work. As soon as they arrived, they each went to their offices and checked their e-mails and incoming telephone calls before attending the scheduled meeting.

The only telephone call Helen had was from Bob Jones, the bowling alley employee that was not working when the detectives were at the bowling alley the day before. He had called Helen, as Loretta Jefferson asked him to do in the message she left him.

After she listened to Jones's call, she started to leave her office, but before she was out of the door, she returned to her desk and placed a call to Jane Midler, the police department spokeswoman. Midler was not in, so she left a message. "Members of the media will probably be calling as soon as you get in. Tell them a white male who had given his name as Ben Zinch but whose true name is Benjamin Barlow was found dead on the floor of Piedmont Bowling. The case is under investigation, and this is the only thing you can tell them at this time. Give them his picture and ask them to request anyone who has any information about him to call the police department."

As soon as she hung up the telephone, she walked over to the interview room where Ken and John were waiting for her. Just as she started to enter the room, Lou Barns joined her.

"Let's see what we have," Helen said as soon as she walked into the room. "Did you get anything of value during your interviews, John?"

"Nothing we don't already know. Not a one of them had seen anyone following the victim out of the bowling alley. None of them knew anything about him, and they all said he never mentioned any relative or friend. None of them saw him after he left the bowling alley," John reported. Helen walked over and poured herself a cup of coffee from their individual-cup coffeemaker, and then walked back to the desk, where she sat on the front edge. She gave them the results of her interview with the bowlers, which was exactly the same as John had reported, except two of her bowlers saw a white man wearing a raincoat and a rain hat follow the victim out of the bowling alley after he was ordered to leave. Neither could furnish any other information, except they thought he was probably about six feet tall.

"Well, Lou," Helen said, after she gave her report, "do you have anything to add to what you told us yesterday about receiving the FBI report which showed his true name is Barlow? And the information you got from Lou Hardy, the guy he robbed a bank with?"

"No," Captain Barns answered. "I went over my notes, and I have no other information. I don't think you can rule out Hardy having arranged to have him killed. I think there is a possibility he knows more than he told me on the telephone. Those are just hunches, and I have nothing to back them up."

"How about the crime scene search, Lou?" Helen asked.

"We found nothing of value there, Helen," he told her. "As you know, there were two steel plates bolted to the wall over a splintered doorway. We dusted the plates and the wrench that was used to remove bottom plate. We found nothing of value between the opening in the wall and where the body was located, except a Colt Police Special .38-caliber revolver. We examined the revolver and the cartridges in the cylinder and found no fingerprints and no DNA. The serial number had been filed off.

"As you also know, there were papers scattered around the office and an envelope containing money was missing. We dusted around everything in the office but found no prints except those of the people who worked there."

Helen stood up and, without saying anything, walked over to where the coffeemaker was. She rinsed her cup out and walked back to join the other detectives.

"What we have," she said, "is the victim's true name." She paused briefly. "I'm inclined to think that in light of the limited information we have, this could be a killing arranged by Barlow's former bank robbery partner, so I think one of you needs to go to Springfield and get as much information about him as you can get. So which one of you wants to go?"

John spoke up. "I'll go, Helen. Ken is due in court this morning. I can be ready to go in an hour."

"Okay," Helen acknowledged. "I'll handle the paperwork for you, John. You go ahead and get out there as soon as you can.

"Since you have to be in court, Ken, I will go over to the bowling alley and talk to the three bowlers and the other employee to see if we can get any more information.

"By the way, Lou and John, I didn't leave Ken out. He told me last night that the bowlers he interviewed came up with nothing, except one of them told him about the white guy who followed our victim out the front door of the bowling alley."

CHAPTER EIGHT

As soon as Helen Martin adjourned the meeting, she got into her car and drove straight to the bowling alley. She had not checked to see what time they would open, but she felt sure at least the manager would be there when she arrived. She was right. There were three cars in the parking lot when she drove in. She parked her car in the space closest to the front door. She got out of the car and walked up to the front door. There was no police officer on duty, but there was a note on the front door telling everyone that the bowling alley would be closed today but would reopen for bowling tomorrow morning at the usual time.

The door was unlocked, so Helen walked in and went straight to the counter, where Jesse Moore and Loretta Jefferson were standing, talking to Bob Jones, the employee she had not met.

"Good morning, Helen," both Jesse and Loretta greeted her.

"Good morning to you," Helen answered. "Loretta, I'm glad you're here. How about calling the last three bowlers on your list and asking them to come to the bowling alley? Since the bowling alley is not open for business, I can see them here rather than have them go to the police department." Then she turned to Bob Jones and said, "You must be Bob Jones?" "Yes, ma'am, I am," he answered.

"Since I haven't had a chance to talk to you yet, how about joining me over at one of the bowlers' tables so we can talk?" she said as she started walking toward the table.

As soon as they were seated, Helen said, "Why don't we start by you telling me everything you know about the murdered man who you knew as Ben Zinch?"

"I really didn't know him," he said. "I met him when he came in two or three weeks ago and asked about bowling in the senior league. The team that was in second place needed a new bowler because one of their members dropped out, and he joined the team. I'm not sure whether or not I saw him again until I heard the argument between him and Mr. Moore. As soon as I heard their raised voices, I started walking over there, but one of the bowlers had stepped in, so I just stood there and watched him leave."

"Did you ever see anyone with him, or do you know any of his friends or relatives?"

"No. I never saw him with anyone. I don't know the identities of any of his friends or relatives."

"A couple of bowlers saw a man wearing a raincoat and a rain hat go out the door right after Zinch, or Barlow, as we now know his true name to be. Did you see that man?"

"Yes, I did. He was at the counter asking for a lane to bowl on, and I told him they were all being used, but one would be available in a few minutes. About that time, the argument between Mr. Moore and whatever-his-name-is started. He stood at the counter and watched them, and then he turned and followed Barlow out the door."

"Can you describe him?"

"Not really. There was nothing unusual about him. He seemed to be about six feet tall. Like you said, he was wearing a raincoat, and he had a hat on to keep the rain off his head. I never really paid much attention to him."

"Do you think you could identify him if you saw him again?"

"I'm pretty sure I could not."

"Okay," Helen said. "I think that's all for now. How about asking Jesse and Loretta to come over?"

"I'll send them right over, Mrs. Martin. I'm sorry I couldn't be of any more help."

"Well," she said, "you can only tell me what you know."

As soon as Jesse and Loretta joined Helen, she asked, "Have either of you learned any information at all that will help us in this investigation? Have you thought of anything you meant to tell me but forgot to?"

Both of them said they could furnish no new information. Loretta told her that she had been able to contact all the three bowlers and that they would be at the bowling alley in a few minutes.

For the next twenty minutes, they talked about nothing in particular, and then the first of the bowlers to be interviewed came in. Loretta met her at the door and took her over to meet with Helen.

As soon as Loretta left them, Helen introduced herself as chief of detectives and went over the case as she had with the other bowlers. When questioned, she provided Helen with the same information as the others had and claimed she had not noticed anyone leaving the bowling alley at the same time the victim did.

By the time Helen finished her questioning, another bowler came in, and she asked her the same questions she had asked the other bowlers she had interviewed. No new information was obtained. Helen, as she had with all the other bowlers, thanked her for taking her time to come in.

After waiting for a few minutes, Gary Jackson, the last remaining bowler to be interviewed, arrived. He was immediately brought over to Helen and introduced to her.

As she had with all the other bowlers she interviewed, she gave him her title and asked if he had any objections to her recording the interview. He did not answer her immediately, and she asked again if he had any objections to her recording the interview.

Jackson answered this time, "I know my rights, and I do not have to talk to you."

"That's true," Helen agreed, "but why would you not want to talk to me? I would think you would want to help us find the person who killed one of your fellow bowlers. That is . . . unless you killed him. Maybe I should give you your Miranda rights."

"I did not say I would not talk to you. I said I knew I did not have to. Of course, I didn't kill him. I did not even know who he was. I don't know anything about him. I don't know any of his friends or relatives, and I never saw him being followed out the door by anyone. I understand that these are the questions you have asked all the other bowlers."

"You're right, Gary, those are the questions I was going to ask you, and I appreciate you setting aside your rights and talking to me. The only other thing I can say is that I think maybe you have been watching too many TV shows. But I appreciate your coming in, and if you should obtain some information that would help us identify the murderer, please call me. Here is my card," she added as she handed it to him.

As soon as Jackson left, Helen walked over to the counter and asked Jesse if he knew Gary Jackson.

"Oh yes," Loretta answered before Jesse could reply. "He's a smartass but is harmless. He can be annoying at times, but all the other bowlers know him and pretty much ignore him."

Just then, Helen's telephone rang. It was the duty officer at the police department.

"You need to come over as quick as you can, Helen. There's a lady here who claims your murder victim is her husband. She says she saw his picture on television, and she is sure it is her husband, but his name is not Barlow or Zinch."

"I'll be there as quick as I can," she assured him. "Keep her there." She turned off her phone, grabbed her briefcase, and started for the door. "We may be getting a break!" she yelled back over her shoulder.

When she got to her car, Helen turned on the siren and emergency lights and drove hard all the way back.

CHAPTER NINE

When Helen Martin arrived at the police department parking lot, she jumped out of her car before it even stopped moving. She quickly entered the building and headed toward the duty officer's window. She saw a woman standing in front of the window, talking to him. She had salt-and-pepper hair and was wearing a pair of faded blue jeans and a denim shirt. She must have rushed straight to the police department as soon as she saw Ben Barlow's picture on the television without taking time to change her clothes, Helen thought. She had obviously been crying.

Helen quickly walked up to the woman and introduced herself. She gently took hold of her arm and led her into her office. When they were inside the office and the woman was seated, Helen asked her if she would like a cup of coffee or a soda, which she declined. Before Helen could say another word, tears started flowing down her cheeks again.

"I know this must be terribly difficult for you, but before I can help you, I need you to talk to me," Helen said. "Can you do that?"

"I'll try," she replied as she dabbed her eyes with the tissue Helen handed her.

"Let's start by you telling me your name, address, and phone number. But first, may I record our conversation?"

"Yes," Maggie answered, "if you want to."

"Thank you," Helen said. "Now, go ahead."

"I am Maggie Yelson. We live at 1621 W. Fourteenth Street, Piedmont, North Carolina," she replied. She paused for a moment, and then she reached into her purse and took out a slip of paper with her cell phone number written on it. She handed it to Helen, who read the number aloud, before returning the paper to her. "I just got a new cell phone, and I haven't memorized the number yet," she explained.

As soon as she had furnished the requested information and without any prompting, she said, "That man the announcer on TV said was murdered at the bowling alley is my husband. I want to see him."

She started sobbing again.

"I am so sorry you had to find out about your husband the way you did," Helen told her as gently as she could. "Let me make a phone call, and then I can take you over to the morgue, and you can identify your husband's body. This will be very difficult for you."

"I know it will be, but I have to see for myself."

Helen picked up the telephone and notified the attendant at the morgue that she was bringing Maggie over.

After Helen hung up the telephone, Maggie said, "I don't understand any of this. Why was my husband killed, and who killed him? And I don't understand why the police are saying this man is Benjamin Barlow, when his name is Ben Yelson."

"Those are things we don't know now," Helen admitted, "but we will find out. Let's walk over to the morgue now, Mrs. Yelson, so you can make sure the deceased is really your husband. Like I said before, I know this will be difficult for you. Is there anyone you would like to go with us?"

"I don't know anyone well enough to ask," she said. "We've only lived here for such a short time. Please, can we go now?"

On the way to the morgue, Maggie stayed quiet. When they arrived at the morgue and started to go inside, Helen could feel her shaking. She put her arm around her and said softly, "This will be hard for you, Maggie, but I will stay with you, and we will get through it together."

Once inside, Helen identified herself and Maggie asked to see the victim. As soon as he was rolled out, Maggie gasped and said in a shaky voice, "He is my husband." Then she started sobbing again, and Helen had to hold her up.

"Is there any doubt in your mind, Maggie?"

"No, I'm sure. If you will look on the inside of his left arm, you will see a tattoo of a pair of dice. Did you see them?" she asked the attendant, who acknowledged that he had.

"Let's step over here, where you can sit down," Helen said as she led Maggie over to an empty chair. "Would you like to be alone for a few minutes?"

"No. I would like to leave," she said. "Will you take me back to your office?"

"Yes, I will. I know this is a terrible time for you, Maggie, but when we get back to my office, I need to get as much information from you as possible. Can you talk to me and furnish me with information that might help identify, locate, and capture the person who killed your husband?"

"I understand," she said. "I'll do everything I can to help get whoever did this."

Helen notified the attendant that they were ready to leave. As she started to walk away, he handed her what appeared to be a wadded up piece of paper. "We found this in one of his pants pockets," he said. "It must've been missed when his clothes were searched earlier."

Helen thanked him and put the paper in her purse without looking at it and returned to where Maggie was waiting.

When they were back in Helen's office, she again offered Maggie something to drink, and this time she requested a cup of coffee with sugar and cream.

After she had a sip or two of the coffee, Helen said, "There are a couple of things that come to my mind immediately. First of all, your husband was not killed just today, and you waited over twenty-four hours without reporting him missing. The other thing is that you told me your last name is Yelson, and yet we know his name is Barlow."

"I don't understand why you keep telling me his name is Barlow when it is Yelson," Maggie said. "I can tell you why I did not report him missing. He is—or was—a financial advisor, and every once in a while, he would have to meet with some important person and would have to stay out overnight without letting me know before he left for the day. He warned me this could happen when we first started living together. He said these meetings would come up unexpectedly, and he wouldn't have time to tell me before he went to meet with them."

Maggie stood up and took her empty coffee cup over to the stand and set it down. She was beginning to look tired.

"Like I said earlier, Mrs. Yelson, I know this is a terrible time for you, but we want to catch the killer as quickly as we can, and we need all the information we can get, so if you can force yourself to talk to me about your husband, it could help a great deal."

Maggie returned and sat down. "I want whoever did this caught. I'll tell you anything I can if it will help," she said in a shaky voice with tears flowing again.

Helen pushed a box of tissues over to her. "Let's continue by you telling me when and where you first met Ben," Helen suggested. She placed a recording device on the corner of her desk near Maggie. "If you don't mind, I would like to record our conversation. This will make sure I get everything you say just exactly right, Mrs. Yelson."

Maggie agreed to the recording but then said, "Please call me Maggie. I met Ben about a year ago in a little town about forty-five or fifty miles south of Richmond, Virginia. I was a waitress and was working the breakfast shift. After we finished the breakfast rush, I decided to go roll a few games at the bowling alley. I was a regular bowler in a ladies' league, and I needed to practice. I was given a lane next to where a man, who I later learned was Ben Yelson, was bowling. After he saw me roll two strikes in a row, he struck up a conversation. We talked as we bowled, and after we finished bowling, he invited me to have lunch with him, and I accepted. By the time we finished, I was in love with him, and I thought he was in love with me, so instead of going home, we went to a movie. When it was over, he took me back to the bowling alley where I had left my car.

"After that, we saw each other every day for about a week, and since my apartment lease was expiring, I moved in with him. He told me he was a financial advisor. Since I was not sure exactly what a financial advisor did, I asked him what he did. He said he was paid to tell people how to spend their money and how to make more money. That's when he told me that there might be times when something unexpected would come up and he might have to meet with a company president or vice president, so if he failed to come home some night, I was not to worry about him, but he would get in touch when he could. This happened a few times, and after the first couple of times, I never worried about him.

"While we lived there, our entertainment was primarily bowling. We would go bowling two or three times a week in addition to my ladies' league, which I bowled one night a week.

"About two months ago, Ben came home one morning and told me he had a hot deal, but we had to move to Piedmont, North Carolina, immediately. Since all our furniture was rented, we hopped in the car, and we've been here ever since."

Maggie stopped talking and asked for a glass of water. Helen gave her a glass, and after she took a few swallows, she set the glass down and continued talking. "I left out something. On the way down here, Ben said he had run into an old friend who was in the same business, and they were forming a partnership. He said he would be working long hours until they could get the company going good.

"Since I didn't know anybody and didn't want to sit home by myself every day, I got a job serving tables. They always seemed to be short of help, so I ended up working just about every day of the week. I got tired of this, so I quit just two days before I saw Ben's picture on TV.

"About three weeks ago, Ben told me he had stumbled upon a seniors' league, and he had joined up. He did seem a little concerned that two men who he thought were brothers might have recognized him, but he guessed they didn't because neither of them ever approached him. I didn't know what difference it made if someone had recognized him, and I actually thought he should have been glad he had seen someone he knew. He didn't say any more about it, so I let it drop.

"The last time he left to go bowling in the seniors' league, he came home mad about something, but he didn't say what. I didn't ask him any questions about it because he gets really upset if I ask him about something he doesn't want to talk about. He would rant and rave and cuss. Anyway, that night we went to bed our usual time. When I got up the next morning, he was gone. I didn't think much about it until I saw his picture on the television this morning. I don't know what happened. He must have gotten up in the middle of the night or something and gone back to the bowling alley. I just don't know."

The tears started flowing again, and Helen passed her the tissues again. Helen had listened quietly while Maggie was talking, not wanting to stop her. When it appeared she was finished, she said, "What about his friends or relatives? Did he ever introduce you to any of them?"

"No, he told me he had no living relatives, that his mother, father, and younger brother were killed in a plane crash a couple of years before I met him. Other than the people he knew where he bowled, I don't know of any friends. I assume he had business acquaintances, but he never mentioned any."

"Let's talk about the name difference, Maggie. You said you are married, and your name is Yelson. Is that correct?"

"Yes it is," Maggie said. "About three weeks ago, I was in a bitchy mood, and I reminded Ben that he told me we would get married after we moved to North Carolina. He said, 'That's a great idea, and I know a JP who is one of my customers. I'll call him and see when he can do it.'

"He started dialing on his cell phone as he walked out the front door. When he came back in, he said that Nick would be over the next morning. I asked him if we didn't need to go to the license bureau or something, and he told me Nick would bring all the necessary papers with him. The next morning, Nick was over, and I signed some papers without reading them. I asked both of them if we didn't need a witness. Nick said he had someone who would sign the papers later as a witness, so I didn't have to worry about it. Then he married us."

Helen was amazed and stunned. How could this woman be so gullible, and how could she best tell her that she is not married and never was? "Maggie, does this Nick have a last name?"

"I don't know it. He just said his name was Nick. I was just happy to get married and never thought anything about it."

Helen walked over to the stand where her individual-cup coffeemaker was. She poured herself a cup and asked Maggie if she would like another cup, which she declined. After pouring her coffee, she walked back and sat down again. She had never been in a position like this before. She had to say something, but how do you tell a woman who had just learned her husband was murdered that the same man had put her through a fake marriage ceremony?

"Maggie, I know of no easy way to tell you this, but you are not married. That marriage ceremony was fake. I am terribly sorry. Do you have any friend or relative we can call to stay with you?"

"No, I don't know anyone here well enough to discuss this. I have a married son who lives in Michigan, but we are not on speaking terms. I'll get by."

"I think that's all for now, Maggie. I'll be glad to drive you home and have an officer drive your car if you would like."

"I can drive myself home," she said. "I will probably stay here for a while. Like I told you, I'm a waitress, and I won't have any trouble getting a job. Ben always seemed to have plenty of money, so there is probably a couple hundred lying around the house somewhere."

Helen walked Maggie to her car and thanked her sincerely for talking to her. Then she returned to her office and checked through the names of the bowlers Loretta had given her. She found two men who had the same last names. She called Loretta and verified that they were brothers. She hung up the phone and stared into space for several minutes. For the first time in twenty years, she wished she had a cigarette.

Her solitude was broken when Ken Matthews called to tell her that he was finished with court. She told him everything Maggie had said and gave him her address. She asked if he was free to do a neighborhood investigation. She was especially anxious to get Nick identified.

Ken agreed to do the neighborhood investigation. She knew if the neighbors could supply any information of value, Ken would get it from them. "We'll meet at eight tomorrow morning," she added.

In the meantime, she had another case that needed some urgent work. "Wouldn't it be nice to have only one case at a time to work, like those TV cops?" she said to no one.

CHAPTER TEN

John Patton woke up at 7:00 a.m. fully refreshed and ready to tackle the job that lay in front of him. He had checked into the hotel the evening before, and after he was settled in his room, he called the prison system and arranged to be picked up at 8:30 a.m. the next day.

Since he had plenty of time before he was scheduled to be picked up, he took his time shaving and then took a long hot shower before he dressed for work. After that, he packed up his luggage, checked out, and went to the hotel restaurant for a leisurely breakfast of bacon and eggs washed down with three cups of coffee. Afterward, he got the morning newspaper and spent the rest of the time in the lobby reading about the local news and sports.

About five minutes before he was scheduled to be picked up, John lay the newspaper down and walked over to the hotel door. Just as he stepped through the door, his transportation pulled up to the curb. He quickly got into the car before traffic backed up behind them. He immediately orally identified himself, and they were on their way to the prison, where arrangements had been made for him to interview Lou Hardy, the prisoner who had previously robbed a bank with Ben Barlow. As soon as he walked through the prison door, the duty officer asked to see his credentials. When they were handed to him, he carefully examined them before handing them back. Then he asked John if he was armed. When said he was not, he arranged for him to be escorted to the room Lou Hardy was being held in.

When the officer opened the door for John to enter the room, he saw Lou Hardy sitting alone at a small table. He walked over to him and extended his hand, and Hardy shook hands with him.

"I'm John Patton, the detective with the Piedmont Police Department who talked with you on the telephone. As I told you then, Ben Barlow was murdered, and I'm trying to find out all I can about him that might help us get a lead on the person who killed him. I know you told me you're glad he is dead, but I have a job to do, and I hope you will help me do it."

"Why should I help you? I think whoever killed him should be given a medal."

"You won't be helping him, Lou—may I call you Lou?—you'll be helping me find a murderer before he kills someone else. Who knows, the next person he kills may be an innocent child, or a young mother, or maybe even a person you know and like."

"Why should I help you?" Lou replied. "I don't give a damn about you or your job. If I talk to you, it will be to help me. What can you do for me?"

"You know I'm not from here and I have no influence here. I could lie to you and make all kinds of promises, but I'm not going to do that. The only thing I can do, and I will, is tell the authorities how much you helped me. That's all I can do."

"Then you might as well go back to where you came from."

"Okay, but before I leave, let me say this. I'm not a psychiatrist, but I think it will give you inner peace if you sit here and tell me all you know about the son of a bitch who did you wrong. If I walk out of here and you stay quiet, you're going to wonder, 'Why didn't I talk to him and let him know exactly what a bastard Ben Barlow was and how he took my share of the money and tried to kill me? Would I have lost all the hate that has festered in me all these years, and would I have helped myself if I had talked to him?'

"I'll admit I'm disappointed. I understand you have been studying accounting. I truly hope that when you get out of here, you will get an honest job and become successful."

Lou Hardy sat there staring into space and saying nothing. Finally, after three minutes of not a word being spoken between the two of them, he looked at John and said, "Just what do you want to know about him?"

"I would like to know about your entire association. I always like to know about people I talk to. I try not to be judgmental. I will think of you as a person who made a mistake, who was mistreated by his partner, and who is paying the penalty for both of you."

"Oh hell, I might as well tell you all I know about it."

"Okay, but before you start, do you have any objections if I record what you tell me so there will be no misunderstanding between us as to what you said?"

"That's all right with me."

John took out a small recorder and placed it on the table between them. "Now," he said, "tell me how you met up with and formed a partnership Barlow."

"I first met Ben Barlow about five or six years ago, when we were both in the pen serving a short sentence for some minor something or other. We got out about the same time, and since neither of us had any relatives who wanted to associate with us, and since we had no money, we held up a service station. After that, we agreed that we would rob banks or any place that had money, and it looked like we could rob and make a clean getaway. We planned to keep out only enough money needed to live on and put the rest in a safe deposit box. We decided to keep on until we had half a million dollars, then we would split up and stop stealing. Once we had the money, we would go back to school and get qualified for a legitimate job. That's pretty much the whole story."

"You want to tell me how many banks or other places you robbed and how much money you saved before the bank robbery that put you in jail?"

"Nope, except for the two banks you know about, my past is history, and it's going to stay that way."

"All right, tell me about your last bank robbery."

"You know about that one."

"I only know about the outcome."

"If that bastard hadn't shot me, we would have made a clean getaway, and it still would not have been solved. We watched that bank for several days, until one day, the armored truck came, and the money was taken inside. After it left, we went in.

"As we went in, we put a printed sign on the front door saying that the bank was closed for inventory and would reopen in two hours. There were only three people working, and we put them in the vault after showing them a device we were carrying that was nothing more than smallpox with some wires sticking out, but we told them that it was a timing device so we needed to work fast. We took all the twenties as well as all the fifties we could carry. Before we left, we told them we had put the timer on the hinge of the door, and if it was opened before twenty minutes passed, the building would blow up. That gave us a good head start. We got to the car and threw the money in the trunk, and as I started to go around the car to get in, John pulled out again and shot me in the legs. Then he jumped into the car and drove away, leaving me on the ground. A short time after he drove away, the bankers came rushing out of the bank and found me. The police got there about the same time, and I was taken to the hospital. The rest, as they say, is history."

"Do you know any of Barlow's relatives or friends?"

"No, all he ever told me was that none of his friends or relatives wanted anything to do with him after he went to prison. He did mention one time that he had a wife who ran off with another man. He never mentioned her name."

"Where's the money now?

"I don't know. It was not put in the lockbox that we rented. The police checked it out because I told them where it was because I wanted that son of a bitch caught. All the money that had been in there was gone, so I guess he still has the money somewhere."

John watched Lou to see his reaction before asking, "Did you have him killed?"

"No, I did not. How could I? I don't know anybody that would do it. And if I did, I have no way to pay him."

"Let's explore that a little. It seems that James Hill, a friend of yours, was released about a month ago. It also seems that he lives about forty miles away from where Barlow was killed. What did you have to promise him if he killed Barlow?"

Lou started to jump up, but then remembered he had been ordered to stay seated, so he sat back down. He turned red and then shouted, "This interview is over! I sat here and answered all your questions and tried to help if I could, and you just tried to trick me to get me to admit to something I just told you I did not do, and I don't appreciate it."

"Let me ask you this, Lou. What would you think if you were me and you just found out that a friend of mine was released from prison just a month before the guy I hate with every bone in my body got killed?"

"I don't know what I would think, but I wouldn't try to trick the guy who was trying to help."

"Okay, but I have to ask you one more time: did you have Ben Barlow killed?"

"No, I did not. But If I thought he would do it and I had some way to pay him for doing it, I would have tried. But Jim would not kill anybody. He's a thief, and not a very good one. He keeps getting caught."

"Oh, one more question, Lou. How much money did you have in that safe deposit box before your last bank robbery?"

"We had $176,000 in that box."

"Do you want to tell me where that money came from?"

"No, we keep all that secret. Wait a minute, I will tell you about one of the robberies. Somehow, and I don't know how, Ben knew that some rather wealthy men were going to be playing a poker game. I think he actually knew one of the men or something, but anyway, he knew where the game was being played, and he managed to get us into where they were playing. We watched them play for a while, and when we were invited to sit in, Ben pulled a gun and said, 'No, thanks. We'll just take the pot.' This was our biggest haul. That was one of our first jobs." Lou was obviously proud of this one.

"Any other you care to tell me about?"

"No, that's all."

John thought for a minute and then handed Lou his card. "Thanks very much, Lou. I appreciate your talking to me, and I will tell the prison authorities that I believe you played it straight with me. You have my card, and I'm sure they'll let you call me if you happen to think of anything that would help us solve this case." Then he called the guard to be let out.

One guard took John to see the warden and another took Lou back to his cell.

John thanked the warden, and in answer to the warden's question, he told him that he did not think Lou had any information of value but that he had answered all his questions to his satisfaction.

After John left the warden's office, a prison guard took him to the airport to catch a plane home. He called Helen, gave her a report, and waited for his plane to depart.

Chapter Eleven

Following her usual routine, Helen Martin awoke at 6:30 a.m. to the chiming of her alarm clock. She got out of bed and spent the next fifteen minutes doing her stretching exercises. When she was all limbered up, she took a quick shower. When she had dried off, she slipped into her undergarments and made her bed before sitting in front of her mirror to brush her hair and put on her makeup. When she was satisfied with her appearance, she slipped into a lavender pantsuit and off-white heels.

On the way out of her apartment, she picked up her hand weapon, concealed it, and walked down to her car. She started it up and headed toward the neighborhood restaurant near the police department, where she met Ken Matthews.

They walked into the restaurant together, and as usual, the waitress placed two cups of black coffee on their table without waiting to be asked. They both ordered their usual breakfast consisting of bacon, eggs, and grits with dry wheat toast. When she returned with their order, the waitress refilled their coffee cups before leaving their table. While they were eating, they talked very little, and when they finished, they each got a cup of coffee to take with them. As soon as they got into their cars, they drove to the police department, where they went into their respective offices and prepared for their eight-o-clock meeting.

At exactly eight o'clock, Ken walked over to Helen's office. As soon as he sat down, she said, "So far, we have very little to work with." She walked over to a chalkboard that she had set up and started writing.

1. An unidentified male body left on the bowling lane nearest the outside wall at Piedmont Bowling

2. We have interviewed employees and bowlers who were there the day before the murder. Results: Learned of an unknown white man wearing a raincoat and rain hat who followed the victim from the bowling alley after he was ejected.

3. We interviewed a woman who said her name was Maggie Yelson who thought she was married to the victim because she was married to him by a man named Nick. Results: She was not married to the victim, whose name is actually Barlow, who said his name was Zinch when he bowled. He told Maggie he thought two bowling brothers recognized him.

4. Neighborhood investigations near the bowling alley and near the home where Maggie lived produced no information of value.

"Did I leave anything out, Ken?"

"Nothing I can think of. We have absolutely no lead on the identity of the killer."

Then Helen thought of the piece of paper the attendant at the morgue given her. She had not read it yet. She flattened out the paper so that she could read it. After she read what was on the paper, she handed it to Ken without saying a word.

Ken read, "'Meet me at closing time tonight. I feel bad about throwing you out and I want to make it up to you. Jesse.' Where did that come from, Helen?"

"It was handed to me by the attendant at the morgue yesterday as I was leaving with Maggie. I didn't have a chance to read it, and frankly, I forgot about it until just now."

"That puts a new light on this, doesn't it?"

"Yes, it does, but it doesn't make a lot of sense. I can't believe Jesse Moore would ask Ben Barlow to come down to the bowling, and then murder him just because he used bad language. Plus, he claimed he had not seen him since he ejected him. I don't remember which employee worked that day, but he never said anything about Barlow coming in around their closing time."

"I agree with you, Helen, but we need to have Jesse come in and talk to us."

"Yes, we do," she said as she picked up her telephone and dialed the bowling alley telephone number.

Jesse answered.

"Good morning, Jesse," Helen said. "Something has come up that we need to discuss with you. Can you come down here and meet me in my office? Something new has come up."

"Sure, but I'm here alone right now. Can you come over here?"

Helen thought for a minute before answering. "I could, Jesse, but I have to go over some notes, and it would be better if you could come here. Can you call in one of your employees to take over while you're gone?"

"I can do that. Earl McNeill will be here in about half an hour. As soon as he gets here, I can come over."

"That's fine, Jesse. Just tell the duty officer who you are, and he'll bring you into my office."

"Okay, I'll see you in a few minutes," Jesse acknowledged.

As soon as Helen hung up the telephone, she notified the duty officer, and in just a few minutes, Jesse arrived and was ushered into her office.

"Have a seat, Jesse," she said as she pointed to a soft leather chair facing her desk. When he was seated, she said, "Something has come to my attention, Jesse, that makes it necessary for me to advise you of your Miranda rights." Then she explained what those rights were. Without giving him a chance to interrupt her, she said, "I thought you told us you never saw Ben Zinch—or Barlow, as we now know his name to be—after you threw him out of your bowling alley until you saw his body on the floor of the bowling alley?"

"Do you think I killed him?" Jesse responded.

"Did you?"

"Hell no, I didn't kill him. Why would I do that? I can't believe you think I killed him. You said you have something new. What's that?"

"You sent him a note asking him to come to the bowling alley at closing time. If he came down there in answer to your invitation, you certainly saw him."

"I didn't send him any message. Why would I do that? What's going on, anyway?"

Helen opened her purse and took out the slip of paper she had received from the attendant at the morgue. "What about this, Jesse?" she asked as she handed him the slip of paper she had put into a vinyl envelope.

Jesse looked at the paper, and a puzzled expression appeared on his face. "I didn't send that to him. I don't how to type, and I have never typed on my computer. I have refused to type on it since the day it was brought into my office. You can ask anybody. I do not type."

"What about an old-fashioned typewriter, Jesse? Do you type on one of those?"

"I don't type on anything."

"Jesse, if I asked McNeill how many times you have typed on your computer, what is he going to say?"

"He's going to tell you the same thing I just told you. I don't type."

"Let's just see what he'll say," Helen said as she picked up her telephone and dialed the bowling alley number. "I'm going to put the phone on speaker, Jesse, and let you hear his response. Don't you say a word."

When McNeill answered the telephone, Helen identified herself and then said, "Earl, I have a question for you. How many times a day would you say Jesse uses his computer keyboard to type different things?"

Earl laughed. "Jesse never touches the keyboard. He has refused to type anything ever since the computer was brought in here. We've tried to get him to learn to use it a few times, and then we finally gave up trying."

"Never?"

"Never," he repeated.

"Thanks, Earl," she said before hanging up.

"Do you have a computer at home, Jesse?"

"My wife does. I've never used it."

Helen picked up her telephone and dialed another number. When it was answered, Jesse recognized his wife's voice but said nothing. Helen identified herself before saying, "Mrs. Moore, I have a reason for asking you this question. How often does Jesse use your computer?"

Mrs. Moore answered, "You say you are a detective? Why are you calling me? What is this all about?"

At this point, Jesse spoke up. "Honey, I'm down at the police station discussing the murder at the bowling alley, and the detective does have a reason for asking you that question."

"Okay, if you say so, but I don't understand why she would care about using my computer, since you don't use it in the first place. Why would she be asking that, since you have never used it? This doesn't make a lot of sense to me."

"Thank you, Mrs. Moore. Jesse will explain it to you when he gets home." She hung up. "Jesse, I'm going to ask you this question one more time. Did you have anything to do with the murder of Ben Barlow?"

"No, I did not."

"Jesse, someone wants us to believe you killed Ben Barlow. Do you have any idea who that could be?"

"No, I can't think of anybody."

"Have you thrown anybody else out of the bowling alley in the last year or two?"

"No. Barlow's the only one I ever told to leave. I've never had any trouble before."

"Were you ever threatened by anyone?"

"No, I can't—wait a minute. About nineteen or twenty years or so ago, my daughter was raped. She testified against him, and he was sent to prison. Right after he got there, he killed himself. About a week later, I got a call from some guy who said he was the rapist's brother, and he said when he got out of jail, he would get me. Since he said he was in jail, I didn't pay much attention to him."

"Didn't you call the police?"

"I told the DA about it, and he said he would look into it, but I never heard from him. He did tell me that he had received a few of those threats, and usually nothing ever comes of them."

"What is his name, Jesse? Where was he imprisoned?"

"I don't remember. I think it was Edward something. I'm not sure."

"What's your daughter's name and address?"

"Her name is Jean Lambert, and she lives at 2583 S. Keystone Avenue here in Piedmont. She's married and has a little girl. Right now she's out of town with her husband, but she will be home later tonight."

"Did she get a threat too?"

"No, she never did."

"Can you think of anything else that might help us get the killer identified, Jesse?"

"No. I think I have told you everything I know, Helen. Am I still a suspect?"

"No more than anyone else involved in this," Helen replied. "Thanks for coming in. I appreciate it. Try to convince your wife we are not crazy."

After Jesse left, Helen said, "Let's get some lunch and then get the brothers in here."

Chapter Twelve

After Helen Martin and Ken Matthews were finished eating, they returned to Helen's office to discuss the information they had just gotten and to plan what they would do next.

They both agreed that Jesse Moore was telling the truth about not having seen the victim after he left the bowling alley until he saw his body the next morning. They were certain he had not typed the slip of paper with the invitation to come to the bowling alley at closing time. But who did? Helen checked the list of bowlers given to her by Loretta Jefferson. She located the telephone numbers for Jack Burton and Hal Burton. Since most of the members were retired, she hoped they would both be home.

First, she called Hal Burton, and when he answered, she identified herself and told him she needed to talk to him again, and he readily agreed to come in and talk to her. Then she called Jack Burton and told him the same thing, and he also agreed, without asking her why, to come in.

While they were waiting for the two men to report in, she and Ken discussed how they would approach the interviews. They agreed to push them and see if they got any information that would help their investigation. They had only waited a few minutes before Jack Burton arrived. Helen greeted him, and then identified herself and Ken Matthews. She pointed to a chair next to where Ken was seated. "Have a seat, Jack."

As he walked over to the chair, he said he knew Matthews since he had talked to him the night before.

After Jack was seated, Helen said, "Mr. Burton, I have received information that indicates you were not truthful last night. Therefore I feel I should tell you of your Miranda Rights."

When she started to explain to him what those rights were, he interrupted her. "I know what my rights are. What are you saying? Do you think I killed Ben Zinch?"

"Did you?" she fired back at him.

"No, I did not. Why would I want to kill him? I didn't even know him. I only saw him a couple of times at the bowling alley."

"I have information that you recognized him, but you said you didn't know him. Why are you hiding the fact that you recognized him?"

"Okay. I don't know what someone has told you, but I told Detective Matthews I do not know him because I don't. He didn't ask me if I recognized him, so I never told him I thought I might have. Twelve or thirteen years ago, my brother and I went with our cousin to see a guy in Charlotte who said he was a financial advisor. He had told my cousin he had a great deal for him, but he had to act fast before the general public found out about it.

"Our cousin asked him to explain the deal to us, and after he did, we told our cousin that he was being taken. Unfortunately, he didn't take our advice and invested $50,000 with him. Of course, his money was gone, and so was the financial advisor. He reported the incident to the authorities, but nothing ever came of it. About six months ago, our cousin was in a car wreck and was killed."

"I'm sorry to hear about your cousin," Helen said before she turned and walked over to the window. She stood there, looking out the window for a few seconds. Then she swung around and faced him. "Is that the complete truth, Mr. Burns?"

"Yes, and please call me Jack."

"Okay, Jack. What did you do between the time Ben Barlow—that is his true name, you know—was told to leave the bowling alley and the time he was found dead in the same bowling alley?"

Jack hesitated. "Ah. Ah. Do I have to tell you?"

"Why would you not tell me? Do you have something to hide?"

"Yes, but it has nothing to do with the murder. Is what I tell you kept in confidence? Will you be talking to our wives?"

"Should I talk to them?"

"No. I mean we spent the night with two other women."

"Do those women have names and addresses?"

"Yes, but you don't have to see them, do you?"

"I don't know. Want to tell me about what happened?"

"My brother and I dated twins in college. After we graduated, they went their ways, and we went ours. We hadn't seen them or heard from them until the night after Barlow was thrown out of the bowling alley. Somehow they had my telephone number and called me. It seems they had divorced recently and had moved to Piedmont and were sharing an apartment. Our wives work for the same company and were out of town on business, so Hal and I went to see them. After a few drinks, we spent the night."

"I need their names and addresses," Helen said.

"You aren't going to contact them, are you?"

"Only if I need to," she said.

"Will you tell our wives?" Jack asked almost in a whisper.

Helen almost felt sorry for him but not much. "I have no intention of telling them. I'm only trying to solve a murder case. Thank you for coming in, Jack. Now will you tell your brother to come in?"

Jack turned and left the room without saying another word. Within seconds, his brother, Hal, came in and was requested to be seated.

As soon as Hal was seated, Helen introduced herself and detective Ken Mathews. Then she followed the same procedure she had followed with his brother and got the same answers.

After Hal Burton left, Helen turned to Ken. "What do you think? Were they truthful?"

"I think they were. They sure picked a bad time to cheat on their wives. They will wonder a long time if we are going to expose them."

"Any time is a bad time to cheat on your spouse. Let them sweat. I agree. I think they told us all they know. Anyhow, that's all for today. John will be back tonight, so let's get together at eight o'clock in the morning."

Helen sighed. "We do so much more work that does not produce any positive results than we do work that does. But if we missed something, all we would hear is 'I would have thought they would have done that first.'"

"It goes with the territory," Ken replied.

CHAPTER THIRTEEN

Helen Martin spotted the killer standing with a group of people outside the library. Without looking at him, she walked straight toward him. When she was ten feet from him, he spotted her and ran. She ran after him, yelling for someone to stop him, but nobody made any effort to help her. Just as she was ready to pounce on him, she woke up. It was all a dream.

Helen had not had a very restful night. Three days had passed, and they still had no knowledge of the identity of the killer. They had obtained a good deal of information regarding the victim, but nothing they had learned about him helped them identify his killer. She shook the cobwebs from her head and slipped out of bed ready to attack the investigation again.

This morning, Helen decided to eat at home, so she took her time getting ready for work. After fixing her hair and putting on her makeup, she decided to wear a pale blue skirt and a white blouse. When she was finished dressing, she drank a cup of black coffee before she poured herself a bowl of cereal, which she ate between sips of her second cup of coffee. When she finished eating, she got into her car and drove to her office, where she prepared for her eight o'clock meeting with Ken Mathews and John Patton, the two other detectives working with her on the case.

Promptly at the scheduled time, both detectives joined Helen in her office. John gave a detailed report about his interview with Lou Hardy. He said he was fairly convinced that Hardy had not arranged for the murder of Ben Barlow, but he thought James Hill, a convict and friend of Hardy's who had been released about a month before the murder, should be interviewed, since he only lived about forty miles from where the murder occurred. Helen agreed with him and asked him to handle the interview.

Next, Helen and Ken told John about interviewing Jesse Moore and learning he had a daughter, Jean Lambert, who was raped about nineteen or twenty years ago by a young man who had a brother in prison for killing a man. She was fourteen at the time. The young man, whose name he could not remember, was convicted after she testified. He was sent to prison and committed suicide the day after he arrived. Later, his brother, whose name Jesse also could not remember, called and threatened him. Helen told them she had called Lambert the night before, and she was coming to her office at nine o'clock to be interviewed.

As soon as their discussion was over, John left to interview James Hill. Helen and Ken each got a cup of coffee from their individual-cup coffeemakers and waited for Jean Lambert to come in. They had not had the first sip of the coffee before the duty officer brought her into Helen's office.

"Good morning, Ms. Lambert," Helen said. "I am Helen Martin, chief of detectives, and this is Ken Mathews, who is also a detective. Please have a seat." She motioned to a chair next to the one Ken was sitting in.

"As I told you on the telephone last night, we still have not identified the person who killed Ben Barlow at your father's bowling alley. When we talked to your father, he told us that about nineteen or twenty years ago, you were raped, and you testified against the man who raped you, and he was sent to prison. He also told us that following the trial and the prison sentence, he received a threatening phone call from a man who said he was the rapist's brother and would get even with him."

While Helen was talking, she noticed tears were starting to flow down Jean Lambert's cheeks. "I will never forgive myself for what I did," she said through her tears.

"I'm not here to judge you, Ms. Lambert. I am not going to ask you about the rape case. That is past history.

I need information that could help us identify the person who killed Ben Barlow, the man whose body was left in your father's bowling alley. I need for you to tell me everything you can about the man who raped you and also his brother."

"Please call me Jean," she said as she attempted to get her emotions under control. "As much as I have tried to forget the incident, if you think it will help identify the murderer, I will tell you everything I can," she said as tears started to flow again.

Helen said nothing for a few seconds. Then she said in a consoling voice, "I'm terribly sorry if I reopened old wounds, Jean, and I wouldn't go into this matter if I didn't think it was necessary. Can I get you anything? A cup of coffee or a glass of water?"

"I would like a cup of coffee with cream and sugar, if you don't mind," Jean answered.

Ken immediately went to the coffee machine and filled a cup with coffee. Then he put a cream pitcher and sugar bowl on a tray with the coffee and carried it to Jean. She added the desired amount of cream and sugar and stirred it while Ken returned everything to the coffee stand.

Helen waited patiently while Jean cooled the coffee and sipped about half a cup. When she set the cup down, she asked, "Where do you want me to start?"

"A good place for you to start would be when you first met—I don't know his name. Before you start, however, if you don't object, I would like to tape our conversation. That way, I can concentrate on what you tell me without having to take notes." She turned on the recording device, and Jean agreed to have the tape made.

"His name was Edward Phillips. I met him nineteen years ago. I was fourteen years old when I first met him. He was working in the ice cream store I stopped in after school three or four afternoons a week. When he asked me how old I was, I told him I was sixteen. We got to talking, and he asked me for a date one day, and I went with him to the movies a few times. I told my parents I was going to visit a girlfriend's house to study. After a short time, I thought I was in love with him."

Helen interrupted. "Did he mention any of his relatives or say where he came from?"

"He said his parents were dead and that the only relative he had was a brother, Ralph. He said Ralph had killed a man in a fight and was in prison and would not get out for a long time."

"Did he tell you how old Ralph was or what prison he was in?"

"He said Ralph was four years older than he was. I think he was in prison in St. Louis, Missouri, but I'm not positive. That's all I know about Ralph."

"Do you know where Ralph is now?"

"No, I don't even know if he is out of prison yet or not."

"That's all for now, Jean. Thank you so much for coming in," Helen said as she stood up. "I know this was painful for you, but what you told us could be very important."

Just as Jean was about to leave her office, Helen thought of something. "Wait a minute, Jean. Do you happen to have a picture of Ralph?"

"I used to have a picture of him and Edward together. I don't know if I still have it or not."

"Please try to find it, will you?"

"Sure. If I find it, I'll let you know"

"Please try. It could be very helpful."

"I will."

After Jean Lambert left, Ken left and returned to his office to call the prison in St. Louis to see what information they had about Ralph Phillips. Helen played the recording of the interview with Jean Lambert, listening carefully for anything she may have missed. Then she sat quietly, trying to analyze the few facts they had.

Twenty minutes later, her telephone rang. It was Jean Lambert, and she was so excited Helen had to ask her three times to slow down so she could understand what she was talking about.

"I just got a letter from someone threatening to rape my daughter Bobbi!" she screamed into the telephone. "It's not signed and I'm scared. Bobbi is not at home."

"Where is she?"

"She's at school. What should I do?"

"How old is Bobbi, and what school does she go to?"

"She is six years old and in the first grade at the Margaret McFarland School."

Helen thought for a moment. "I'm going to send a uniformed officer to pick you up and then take you to the school to pick up your daughter. While you are waiting for the officer to get to your house, call the school and have your daughter wait for you in the principal's office. After both of you are in the car, he will bring the two of you to my office. Bring the letter and the envelope with you. Don't handle either any more than necessary. After you get here, we will decide what action we can take."

"I will do that, but have him hurry."

Ten minutes later, Helen got a call from Jesse Moore, who was equally excited as Jean had been. After Helen got him calmed down, he told her he had just received a letter that was not signed and said, in part, "You are next."

"Stay where you are, Jesse, and Ken Matthews will be there as soon as he can get there. Don't handle the letter any more than you have already," Helen instructed.

"Tell him to hurry."

"He's on his way, Jesse," Helen assured him and buzzed Ken and told him about both letters.

Ken told the prison officer he was talking with that something had come up and he would get back with him later. Then he left to see Jesse.

CHAPTER FOURTEEN

John Patton left the meeting, got into his car, turned on his GPS, and headed for the home of James Hill. After driving 43.6 miles over paved roads, his direction instrument instructed him to turn right onto a gravel road. He drove 0.9 miles on this gravel road through a wooded area until he finally came to a log cabin protected by a fenced-in yard.

John drove up to the front gate. When he stepped out of the car, he was met by a large dog charging toward him. He jumped back into the car, not trusting the fence to hold the dog back. He honked the horn a couple of times, but James Hill did not come out of the house. Then he turned on the loudspeaker and announced, "This is John Patton, detective, Piedmont Police Department. Please come out to the car, Mr. Hill, and control your dog."

In response to the request, the front door of the house opened. A man John recognized from his mug shot as James Hill walked out toward the gate.

"Do you have a warrant?" Hill asked, as he approached the gate.

John got out of the car again in order to meet him. "No, Mr. Hill, I do not have a warrant. I only want to talk to you about your friend Lou Hardy."

"What do you want to know about Lou? Did he break out of jail or something?"

"No, nothing like that," John replied. "Why don't you control your dog so we can sit on the porch, where we can be comfortable and have a chat?"

"Did you say you were a detective? Show me some identification."

John took out his credentials and handed them to him.

After Hill examined them, he handed them back. He took hold of the dog's collar and opened the gate. "I might as well talk to you and get it over with. I'm sure if I don't, you'll threaten me with all sorts of things."

"Why don't we make this a friendly conversation?" John said. "I need some information to help us solve a murder case, and you may be able to help me. That's the only reason I'm out here."

"Okay," Hill said, as he released the dog. He walked over to John but did not display any hostility.

Jon reluctantly and carefully petted the dog's head. "What's his name?"

"His name is Patrol. That's what he does. He's not a vicious dog, but he is big and everybody is afraid of him. This gives me a sense of security."

When they reached the porch, John took one chair and James Hill took the other. After they were seated, John took out a battery-operated recording device, turned it on, and held it in his hands. "Do you mind if I record our conversation, James—may I call you James?"

"That's all right with me. You mentioned a murder. Who was murdered?"

"The guy who shot Lou Hardy after he and Hardy robbed a bank. His name was Ben Barlow."

"I didn't know the guy had a name," James said as he laughed. "I thought it was sort of a bitch or bastard."

John laughed too. "I think I would feel the same way if my partner in crime shot me and ran off with my money. Did Hardy discuss him with you very often?"

"Almost daily. I didn't know anyone could hate someone like Lou did that guy. You must've talked to Lou, or you wouldn't be here, so you know the story."

"Yeah, it seems they robbed a bank together, and Barlow shot him on the way out of the bank."

"And the money he got away with has never been found. According to Lou, there's two or three hundred grand out there somewhere that belongs to him," James added. "I can tell you this, Mr. Detective, if Barlow hadn't been killed, Lou would have searched the entire country and killed him after he got out."

"Did Lou ever talk about getting someone to hunt Barlow down and kill him?"

"Not really. Every once in a while he would say he wished he knew someone who could find that bastard and give him what he deserves. Problem was, he didn't know anybody who would take on the job, and he didn't have any money to pay him if he did know someone."

Watching Hill closely, John said, "Did you kill him, James?"

"Hell no, I didn't kill him. I steal things. I don't kill people, and no, he never asked me to do it."

"Do you have any idea who killed Ben Barlow?"

"No. I don't have any idea, and frankly I don't care. Anybody that would do what Ben Barlow did to his friend deserved to meet an untimely death."

"Did Lou ever mention a wife or girlfriend who he thought may have met up with Barlow and ran off with him?"

"I never heard him say whether he was married or ever had been."

"James, you know I have to ask you this. Where were you on the night of October twenty-second?"

"I was in Indianapolis, Indiana, visiting my brother, and I can prove it." He stood up, walked over to a cabinet, and pulled open a drawer. He reached into the drawer and pulled out some American Airlines papers, showing his flight from Charlotte to Indianapolis and return. He handed them to John. "I just got back three days ago." Then he gave John his brother's name, address, and telephone number.

John examined the papers which showed he had been gone for ten days. He thanked James and handed him his card and asked him to call if he came up with any information on the killer. He turned off his recorder and stood up to go. When he did, Patrol stood up too.

"He won't bother you, Mr. Detective. He would like his head petted."

John cautiously petted his head again, and Patrol escorted him to the gate. When he got into the car, he texted Helen to give her the report on James Hill, but she did not answer his text.

CHAPTER FIFTEEN

In exactly one hour from the time Helen Martin received the call from Jean Lambert, Officer Floyd Bennett had her and her daughter, Bobbi, picked up and driven to the office. Jean was still shaking, and when she saw Helen, she rushed over and threw her arms around her and held tight.

After a short time, Helen gently removed Jean's arms and led her to a chair. Jean sat in the chair and pulled Bobbi close to her. After she was seated, she gained her composure, and looking straight at Helen she said, "I'm sorry, but I'm scared."

"I'm sure you are, Jean," Helen replied. "I would be too." Then Helen took the paper bag that Jean was holding. From it she removed the threatening letter and the envelope it came in with a pair of tweezers. She carefully worked them into a vinyl envelope. After she had the letter fully protected, she read it. It read, *I know where you live. I know your daughter is named Bobbi and that she walks to school. I'm not going to tell you when, but when you least expect it, she will know what real rape is.*

Helen then examined the envelope and noted that it was mailed in Piedmont. Then she placed both the letter and the envelope on her desk. "Has anyone touched the letter besides you, Jean?"

"No. I'm the only one that touched it, but before I realized what it was, I handled it like any other letter, so my fingerprints will be all over it."

"I understand, but since your fingerprints are on it, we will need a set of your fingerprints for elimination purposes. We'll get that done when we finish here. Of course, the envelope has been handled by many people, so a fingerprint examination would be of little value.

"When I talked to you earlier, you told me about a Ralph Phillips, who you said was the brother of Edward Phillips, the man who raped you. Do you have any idea when Ralph got out of prison, if he has gotten out, and do you have any idea at all where he might be now?"

"I do not know anything at all about Ralph Phillips except Edward told me he was in jail for killing a man. That was twenty years ago."

"Jean, does your husband, Charles, know about this?"

"Yes, I called him. He is in Seattle on business and will return as soon as he possibly can. I told him that I was being picked up along with Bobbi and was being brought here for protection. He's also familiar with the rape case. And before we go any farther, I think I should tell you about what led up to the trial in which Edward was tried and convicted."

Helen interrupted. "Bobbi, I'm going to call a nice lady, and she's going to take you downstairs and then take you next door to the ice cream store where you can have whatever you would like. How would you like that?"

"Great," Bobbi answered as she jumped up from her chair. "I love ice cream."

Helen picked up her phone and called one of the female employees and told her that she had a little girl in her office who would love to go next door and get some ice cream. When she hung up the phone, Helen said, "Now Bobbi, stay right there for a minute, and Miss Molly will be right in here to take you to get that ice cream."

"Where's that little girl who wants ice cream?" Molly said as she came bursting into the room and looked over toward Bobbi.

"I'm here," Bobbi said, as she ran over to join Molly, who took her by the hand and led her out the door.

"Now Jean, what do you want to tell me?"

"I have been ashamed of what I did for almost twenty years, and I will never get over it," she said. "When I was fourteen, I was very wild. I guess you could say I was really uncontrollable. As I told you, I went by the ice cream store and talked to Edward Phillips about every day. Then one day, my parents went on a business trip and were not supposed to be home for three days. Someone had been hired to stay with me, but they never showed up. The day they left, I went by the store and practically forced Edward to take me to the movies. After the movie was over, I took him home with me, and I practically dragged him into my bedroom and threw myself at him, and we had sex. I was not a virgin. The same thing happened the next day, only my parents came home a day early. When my dad opened my bedroom door, I screamed—not because I was being attacked, but because we were caught having sex.

"My father started yelling and attacking Edward. Edward grabbed his clothes, pushed my father aside, dressed quickly, and ran out the front door. Before I could stop him, my father called the police and told them that I had been raped, and they arrested Edward. Nothing I could do or say convinced my father to not take legal action. When I was forced to testify, they would not let me say it was my fault. I was five days short of being fifteen years old when we were caught.

"After I testified, my father testified that when he opened my bedroom door, I screamed and claimed I was being raped. Edward was convicted of some charge, I'm not quite sure what it was, and he was sentenced to prison, where he committed suicide the day after he got there. I have never been very close with my father since that time."

"What about your mother?" Helen asked.

"My father and mother divorced shortly after the trial, and my father later remarried. My mother and I are close, and we visit back and forth."

"Is your husband aware of all this?"

"Yes, he knows the whole story, and before you ask me, he is the father of Bobbi."

"I am very sorry about your problem," Helen said. "But from what you've told me, and what it says in the letter, it would seem that Ralph Phillips is a person of interest. Twenty years is a long time, and you probably would not recognize him if you saw him, but have you seen anyone, male or female, lounging around, walking back and forth in front of your house or driving back and forth in front of your house? Or has anyone rented a nearby house where they can see every move you make?"

"No, I have not seen anyone that I did not know around the house. I've not received any strange calls, and as far as I know, no one has rented a house near me."

"Has Bobbi mentioned anyone talking to her that she didn't know?"

"No, she hasn't. I think she would have told me if any strange man talked to her."

Just then, Bobbi and Molly tapped on the door. Helen motioned for them to come in, and when they were back inside her office, she thanked Molly for helping out.

Bobbi was still holding a half-eaten ice cream cone. Helen handed her a couple of paper towels as she sat down in the chair next to her mother. She continued eating her ice cream cone.

"Bobbi," Helen said, "has any man or woman that you didn't know talk to you in the last few days when you walked to school or stood in the yard?"

"Yes, ma'am."

"When did that happen?"

Bobbi seemed to be thinking. "I was in the front yard playing with my new puppy. I think it was the day after that man was killed at the bowling alley. Some man walked up to the gate and asked me my name. I told him it was Bobbi." Then she slid out of her chair and threw what was left of her ice cream cone in a nearby wastebasket.

"Did he say anything else, Bobbi?"

Bobbi started to twist and turn and took hold of her mother's hand.

Helen waited patiently before softly asking, "What else did he say, Bobbi?"

"Well, he said, 'I'll bet your mama's name is Jean, isn't it?' I told him it was. Then he said, 'Thank you, Bobbi, you're a nice little girl.'"

Helen looked over at Jean, who looked like she was trying to say something before she passed out.

Helen quickly obtained an ammonia capsule, broke it open, and waved it under Jean's nose. She immediately responded and said to Bobbi, "You never told me about that!"

"I forgot, Mama."

"Bobbi, have you ever seen the man before anywhere?" Helen continued after making sure Jean was all right.

"No, but he seemed like a nice man."

"If I showed you a picture of him, would you recognize him? Could you tell me if he was the same man whose picture I showed you?"

"I don't know, I just saw a little while. He wore glasses."

"Can you tell me how tall he is, or how he was dressed? Do you know how old he is? Was he a white man or a black man?"

"I don't know," Bobbi replied. "He was a white man, and he was about as tall as daddy, but I don't think he was as big as daddy. But I don't know how old he was. He did have a cap that had an airplane on it, but that's all I remember. Is he a bad man?"

"I don't know, honey," Helen said. "I'm going to try and get a picture so you can tell me if it's a picture of the man who talked to you. Can you do that?"

"I don't know, but I'll try."

Helen excused herself and picked up her telephone and called the prison in St. Louis. When she had one of the officers on the line, she explained that one of the detectives had talked to someone there earlier about a former inmate with the name of Ralph Phillips.

"I'm Doug Jackson, and I was the one who talked to him."

"Do you have a mug shot of Phillips?"

"Yes, we do. After I talked to your guy, I checked, and we have a photo of him taken ten years ago when he was released."

"Can you fax a copy to me right away? I need to show it to a person who probably won't stay here long."

"Give me your fax number and I'll send it now."

Helen gave him the fax number and hung up.

"Now, while we're waiting," Helen said, "I want you to initial and date the back of this letter that you received through the mail today." She slid the letter just far enough from its protective cover for Jean to initial and date. Then she did the same thing with the envelope.

"Now, Jean, do you have any plans? I feel sure you do not want to return to your house with Bobbi, and although we can give you temporary protection, we simply cannot do it as an ongoing thing. I think there is a good likelihood that the man Bobbi talked to is the letter writer. If he is, that means he's here in Piedmont, and we don't know what his next actions will be."

Jean said, "No, I do not want to go back to the house. My husband's brother Jim is a pilot who owns his own airplane. Charles was going to call him and see if he would pick me and Bobbi up at a small private airport near here and take us back to his house in Ohio. Let me call Charles, and I'll see what arrangements he has made."

Jean reached in her purse and took out her cell phone and called her husband. She asked him if he had been in touch with his brother, and if he had, what they have decided. He told her that he had been in touch and that Jim would be at the airport in about three hours. He also told her that since he could work from anywhere, he was going to his brother's house instead of returning to Piedmont and would meet them there.

After she hung up the phone, Jean furnished this information to Helen, who had been watching for mug shots while Jean was on the telephone.

Just as Jean turned off her cell phone, Helen's fax machine turned on, and the photo of Ralph Phillips came in. Helen took it and three other photos she had rounded up, mixed them up, and asked Bobbi if any of them was the man she had talked to. Bobbi looked carefully at each photo and pointed to the photo of Ralph Phillips.

"I think that's the man I talked to, but I'm not sure. I know it's not any of the others."

"How sure are you, honey?"

"I'm kinda sure, but I can't be real sure."

"That's fine, Bobbi. You did a good job. Now, why don't you stay where you are for a while so your mother and I can talk about taking you on an airplane ride? You're going to visit your uncle Jim and his family for a while. How would you like that?"

"Oh, I love flying in Uncle Jim's airplane."

"Okay, Jean, we have about three hours to get you and Bobbi ready to move. This is what we can do. I will drive you to your house with a uniformed officer following us. When we get there, we will look for any signs of forced entry, and if we find none, both the officer and I will go into the house with you and Bobbi. You can pack your clothes. Pack what you think you will need for a few weeks, and you may want to take some of your husband's clothes also because right now we do not know how long it will take to solve this matter. We could get lucky and solve it tomorrow, or a year from now it could still be pending. We will do the very best we can. Does this plan sound all right to you?"

"Yes, we can pack, and then will you take me and Bobbi to the airport? I don't want to drive our car out there because I don't know how long it would have to stay there."

"Yes, I will drive you and Bobbi, and both the officer and I will stay there until you are on the plane and in the air."

"Thanks, Helen. I think that's a good idea".

"We have one more thing to do, Jean. We need to get you fingerprinted."

Picking up her telephone, Helen called for one of the technicians to fingerprint Jean. When he came in, he escorted her to where he could take her prints, and when he finished, he returned with her to Helen's office.

Upon their return, Helen took Jean and Bobbi to their house with the uniformed officer following. When they got to the house, they found no evidence of anyone trying to break in, so they went into the house, and Jean started packing.

It took Jean about an hour to pack up what she felt she absolutely had to take with her. After that, they put the clothes in Helen's car and started for the airport. Helen stayed in touch with the officer who was following them, and he never detected anyone attempting to follow them.

After they arrived at the airport, they waited for about an hour for Jim to arrive. As soon as he set down, he refueled, loaded Jean and Bobbi into the plane with their clothes, and took off for Ohio.

Once they were airborne, Helen and the uniformed officer returned to the police department.

CHAPTER SIXTEEN

Detective Ken Matthews rushed over to Piedmont Bowling, where Jesse Moore was waiting for him. As soon as Ken walked up to the counter, Jesse, whose hands were trembling, attempted to hand him the letter he had received in the mail.

"Lay the letter on the counter, Jesse," Ken instructed, and then with the use of tweezers, he slid the letter into the vinyl envelope. When the letter was protected, he took the same tweezers and pulled the letter back out just far enough to let Jesse initial and date it on the back side. Then he pushed it back into its protective covering. He did the same thing with the envelope. After the letter was properly initialed, dated, and protected, Ken read it. It contained only three words: *You are next.*

"When did you get this letter, Jesse?"

"I got it in today's mail, which arrived about an hour ago."

"Was it sent here or to your home address?"

"It was sent to my home address. I met the mail carrier as I was leaving to come to work, but I didn't open it until I got here."

"That means the letter writer knows where you live. Has anyone else touched this letter, Jesse?"

"No. I'm the only one who has handled it. My fingerprints will be all over it because I didn't realize what type of letter it was when I first opened it."

"That's okay, Jesse, but we will have to get a set of fingerprints from you for elimination purposes.

"Have you seen anyone loitering around your house that you did not recognize in the last few days, or did you notice anyone driving slowly past your house? Did you notice any car you thought might be following you home at any time in the past few days?"

"No, to all that."

"How about here at the bowling alley, Jesse? Have you noticed any strangers, especially any who seem to be paying more attention to you than to their bowling?"

"Well, we see strangers here every day. People who don't bowl here regularly, they rent shoes, get a lane assigned to them, find a bowling ball, and then bowl. We do this so often we pay little attention to them."

"Do you have any idea who might have mailed this letter to you? Other than the person who was murdered here a few days ago, have you had a run-in with anyone?"

"No. Other than that one incident, we have had no problems at all. The only person I can think of is the brother of the guy who raped my daughter who was in jail at the time for murder. I told you or the other detective about getting a threatening call from him, but that was twenty years ago."

"Well, we can't rule him out, Jesse. Some people carry a grudge forever. I've talked to the prison authorities in St. Louis, where he was incarcerated, and he was discharged ten years ago. 'Course we are going to try to locate him. I don't know how long that will take or even if we ever find him. What are you going to do while we work the case, Jesse? Do you want to hide, or are you going to keep working? What action are you going to take?"

"I'm going to keep working like I always have. I have a permit to carry a concealed weapon that I keep under the counter. From now on, though, I will keep it on me."

"How much training have you had with this gun, Jesse?"

"I know how to use it. I was a marine for four years when I was in my twenties. I haven't forgotten what I was taught. I wouldn't mind if an officer dropped in every once in a while, but I know you cannot give me round-the-clock protection."

"That's right, Jesse. I wish we could, but that's simply out of the question. I will have a uniformed officer drop in two or three times a day and in the evening for the next few days. We are going to do our best to find whoever wrote this letter to you. Also, you probably don't know this yet, but your daughter also received a threatening letter today. Helen Martin was going to interview her, but I don't know the results yet or what she plans to do."

As soon as Jesse heard his daughter Jean Lambert had received a threatening letter, he picked up the phone and called her house number. When he got no answer, he started to come out from behind the counter. "I'm going over there," he said.

"Wait a minute, Jesse. Wait till I get back to the station, and when I find out what she's going to do, I will let you know. Right now she's probably with Helen Martin and is perfectly safe. You being over there won't help, and you would probably be in the way. Better still, let me call Helen now, and I'll see what I can find out for you."

Before Jesse could respond, Ken got in touch with Helen. "I'm here with Jesse," he told her, "and he wants to know what Jean is going to do."

Helen told him the plan, and he passed it on to Jesse.

"So you see, Jesse, if you go there, you could slow down her departure, and she wants to leave as quickly as possible. I know you would like to see them because they are your daughter and granddaughter, but right now you need to think of them."

Jesse thought about it and then said, "You're right, of course. I'll wait and call her later tonight. You probably know we haven't been close since the trial that sent the man who raped her to prison, but she is still my daughter, and I still love her, as well as my granddaughter."

"You're doing the right thing, Jesse. Their safety comes first."

Jesse finished coming from behind the counter and told his employee, "I am going home. You can close up tonight and open in the morning. I don't think you're in any danger, since whoever this person is, he's only interested in me."

As Jesse started to walk away, Ken walked beside him. "That's all we can do here, Jesse, but I want to follow you home and talk to your wife to see if she's talked to any strangers recently or has seen anybody loitering around your house or has noticed anyone driving slowing past your house."

About thirty minutes later, they arrived at Jesse's home, and Ken went inside with him. Jesse introduced him to his wife Irene and told her about the letter he had received.

After the introduction was made, and Ken got her quieted down, he asked Irene Moore the same questions he had asked Jesse.

When she could furnish no information of value, he thanked her and asked Jesse to stop by the police station to have his fingerprints taken within the next day or two.

Since he was finished here, Ken returned to his car, got in, drove back to the police station, and resumed his conversation with the officer at the prison department.

CHAPTER SEVENTEEN

As was their practice during a joint investigation, detectives Ken Matthews and John Patton entered the office of their chief, Helen Martin, at exactly 8:00 a.m. to discuss their progress in the investigation to date. Without wasting any time with preliminary greetings, she waved them over to where they usually sat when in her office.

"We've got a lot to cover," she said. Then without waiting for either of them to reply, she went into detail about her interview with Jean Lambert and her six-year-old daughter, Bobbi. She also reported Jean's decision to move into her brother-in-law's house in Ohio until the case was solved. Then she laid the protected letter she had gotten from Jean on the table for both detectives to read. As soon as she laid the letter on the table, she walked over to their coffeemaker and brewed herself a cup of black coffee. As she walked back to her desk, she said, "Give us a report on your interview with Jesse Moore yesterday, Ken."

Ken immediately put the protected letter he had received from Jesse on the table. Then he narrated the details of the interview with Jesse and Jesse's decision to keep working while wearing his concealed handgun at all times. He pointed out that Jesse had a concealed gun permit.

When Ken was finished, Helen brought out the whiteboard and entered the new information. When she had it up to date, they discussed this new information and how to use it to further their investigation. When they finished their discussion, they all were in agreement that Ralph Phillips was probably the letters' writer and the murderer of Ben Barlow, and that he was probably living in the area.

Helen picked up both letters from the table. "I'll send both letters to our laboratory to see if they can come up with any fingerprints or DNA. Also, as you both know, if we come up with a suspect printer, the laboratory may be able to determine if that particular printer printed the letter in question. I really don't expect to be lucky enough for them to find either fingerprints or DNA, but maybe we'll get a break. We sure have nothing to lose."

Helen put the letters on her desk and turned and walked toward the door. "Take a break, guys. I've got to get rid of some of this coffee. Be back in a minute."

As soon as the door closed, Ken turned to John. "Be ready to hit the road, John. I think, as soon as I give my report, we will both be traveling."

"Why? What did you find out when you called the prison?"

"Wait until Helen returns, and I'll tell both of you at the same time."

"How did you make out with your interview with James Hill?" Helen asked John as soon as she entered the office.

"I talked to him for a quite a while, and during that time, I became convinced he had nothing to do with the killing of Ben Barlow. And this was before he showed me ticket receipts from American Airlines that showed he was in Indianapolis, Indiana, during the time Barlow was murdered. I put all the details in my report including my meeting up with Patrol, his big watchdog."

Of course, when he mentioned his meeting with Patrol, both Helen and Ken wanted to hear about it. At first he told them to read his report, but when they kept after him, he told them the whole story, making Patrol sound both twice as big as he was and twice as vicious. Both laughed so hard they shook.

"I sure wish I could have seen you jump back into the car," Ken said during his laughter. "I bet you opened the door while you were in midair," Ken said while still laughing.

"Yeah, if you had been there, you would have beat me through the door."

"Okay," Helen said, trying to stop laughing, "back to work. I am glad you didn't get hurt and you did not shoot the dog, John."

Helen turned to Ken. "Give us what you got from the prison officer, Ken. You were on the phone for over an hour."

"Ralph Phillips was released from prison about ten years ago after having served a lengthy sentence for murder. He was required to wear an ankle monitor for three years. He reported monthly as required, and he made no attempt to remove the monitor. During those three years, he worked as a cook at one of the better restaurants. Apparently, he had learned to cook during his prison stay. At the end of the three years, the monitor was removed, and he left the area without letting anyone know where he went. Two and a half years later, he turned up in Portland, Maine. He had married a woman by the name of Sarah Abrams about eight months earlier under his true name. When Sarah was found murdered, he was questioned and fingerprinted but never charged with her murder.

"When they remembered that Sarah's previous husband had also been murdered, Ralph Phillips became a suspect in that murder also. I set out in my report how he approached Sarah, how he got her to marry him, and how he got her to take a life insurance policy on herself, making him the beneficiary.

"Three year later, the same thing happened. This time it was in Walla Walla, Washington. It seems the woman he had married about a year and a half earlier had been murdered. Again he was questioned and fingerprinted but never charged. It was also shown that in the Walla Walla case, as in the Portland case, her husband had been murdered three months before she was."

Helen Martin thought for a moment and then said, "John, you have to be in court today, don't you?"

"Yes, I do. I'm the first witness."

"Well, in that case, Ken, can you go to Walla Walla and see what you can dig up about Ralph Phillips? Especially something showing he is now in our area. Maybe you can even get a better photo than the mug shots we have."

"Yes, I can," Ken replied, "but it is our thirteenth wedding anniversary, and I would like to delay leaving until the first flight out in the morning. My wife has made reservations for dinner and for us to see a play that we have been wanting to see for some time. I can use the rest of today catch up on some of my other cases."

"Sure, that will be fine," Helen answered. "I had forgotten this is your anniversary. Why don't you take the rest of the day off and get ready for a nice evening?"

"I would like to, but as you're aware, I've got some other cases needing attention, so I will work on them until at least late in the afternoon."

"Fine. Happy anniversary. I'll see you when you return. Margaret will make your reservations."

CHAPTER EIGHTEEN

After Helen prepared the two letters for the state lab to check for fingerprints and DNA, she sat quietly at her desk thinking about the case. She mentally rechecked everything that had been done and everything yet to be done. She got out each report Ken and John had submitted and read them again. When she was finished reading their reports for about the third time, she got up from her desk and commenced pacing back and forth across her office. After about ten minutes, she could think of nothing left undone.

Then she remembered. No one had checked with the local motels to see if anyone using the name of Ralph Phillips had stayed at their motel at any time during the week before the murder. Since there were only six motels in the area to be contacted, Helen decided to contact the motel managers in person rather than by telephone. This way, the manager could have the records checked, probably while she waited. Helen got lucky. Not only was every manager at his desk, he was able to have the records checked while she sat there. Not a single motel had a record of anyone being registered under the name of Ralph Phillips during the week before the murder. After Helen finished with her inquiries at the motels, she decided to drive out to Jean Lambert's house. She wanted to know if anyone had attempted to enter the house, or if someone had actually gotten in. Also, she wanted to discuss the matter with Jean Lambert's neighbor. Jean had told her, while she was packing her clothes, that her neighbor's name was Pat Hopkins and that Pat was with her when she got the threatening letter. She had also said that Pat was a close friend.

When Helen arrived at the house, she parked her car in the driveway and walked over to the neighbor's house and rang the doorbell. When the woman who opened the door acknowledged that she was Pat Hopkins, Helen identified herself and said she would like to talk to her.

She was immediately invited to come into the house.

When they were seated, Helen said, "Ms. Hopkins, I was told that you were with Jean Lambert when she received a threatening letter."

"Yes, I was, and please call me Pat."

"Okay, Pat, what happened?"

"Jean and I were standing on her front porch when the mailman handed her a letter. She opened it without paying any attention, and then she started screaming.

The whole neighborhood could have heard her, but I guess nobody was home.

"Anyway, I finally got her calmed down and into the house. I kept asking her what happened. She said that someone was going to rape Bobbi. I reached for the letter. Jean yelled, 'Don't touch it, don't touch it.' Then she called you. I stayed with her until the policeman got here."

"Did you touch the letter, Pat?"

"No, I didn't."

"Did she tell you anything about the background leading up to the letter?"

"No, that's all that was said about it. She did ask me to watch after the house, since it would be empty for an unknown period of time. She called me this morning. She said she was not going to tell me where she was because she thought it was best that I didn't know. I figured this had something to do with the man who was murdered in her father's bowling alley, but I never asked her any questions. She sounded really frightened."

"She is frightened, and she has good reason to be. I can't go into the details, but I would like for you to watch the house and let me know if anyone, especially a man, comes around. Don't approach him yourself, but give me a call." Then she handed Pat her card.

Pat examined the card she was given before saying, "I did see a man over there yesterday evening, about five o'clock. He seemed to be trying to get the front door open, but then he gave up and walked around the house. He looked in a couple of windows as he went by them. Then he walked back out to the street, turned right, and walked away. I don't know where he went, and I never saw him get into a car."

"Can you describe this man?"

"He looked pretty much like any normal man. He appeared to be about six feet tall and weighed between a hundred and eighty and two hundred pounds. I couldn't see his hair because he had on a baseball cap. He was wearing blue jeans and a red checkered shirt. Normally I would not have paid any attention to him."

"I'm going over to check the house now, Pat. How about walking over there with me?"

"Sure, I'll be glad to."

As they started walking over to the house, Helen stopped by her car and took out a photo of Ralph Phillips. She handed it to Pat. "Is this the man?"

"I can't really tell," she said after looking at the photo for several seconds. "I couldn't see him that close. Oh, there is one other thing. He was wearing what appeared to be leather gloves, although it wasn't cold. I just assumed they were driving gloves or something and didn't give it much thought."

Helen thought for a minute and then said half under her breath, "Well, so much for prints."

Helen walked with Pat up to the front door. She tried to open the door, but it was locked. Then she and Pat walked around the house, checking the windows, and when they got to the back door, she tried to turn the doorknob, but the door was locked. They completed their walk around the other side of the house but saw no broken windows or no tool marks. After they finished checking the house, Helen thanked Pat before getting into her car and driving over to Maggie's apartment.

Helen really expected Maggie to be gone, but since she was going right past her apartment, she decided to stop and see. She was pleased when Maggie answered the door.

Maggie acted surprised to see her but grabbed her hand and pulled her into the house before she had a chance to say anything.

"I'm really glad to see you," she said. "I got great news today."

"What kind of news? Is it something that will help our investigation?"

"No. No. I got a call from a lawyer asking me to come to his office. He said he had great news for me, but I needed to come to his office. I tried to get him to tell me what it was over the telephone, but he wouldn't do it, so I went downtown to his office. He said an uncle I didn't even know I had died and left me close to a quarter of a million dollars."

"That is good news," Helen replied. "Have you gotten the money yet?"

"Yes, he handed me a check for $238,000. As soon as I got it, I took it down to the Third National Bank and opened an account, but they told me I can't draw any money out until the check clears. When it does, I'm going to take it all out and put it in a safe deposit box. Then if something happens to the bank, I'll have the money."

"I don't think that's a very good idea, Maggie. You won't earn any interest on your money."

"Well, the bank is not paying much interest anyway, and I like to have it where I know I can go down and take it out as I need it."

"Well, that's up to you, Maggie, but if I were you, I'd get some financial advice."

"Well, I don't trust financial advisors either. You know, I was married to one, or at least he told me he was, so how do I tell a real financial advisor from a phony one?"

"That's a good question," Helen replied. "After your check clears, get in touch with me, and I'll help you find someone reliable."

"Yeah, I might do that. Now I was so excited about getting this money that I forgot to ask you about your investigation. Do you know who killed Ben yet?"

"I don't know, Maggie. We may have some pretty good leads. Does the name Ralph Phillips mean anything to you?"

"No, I never heard that name before."

"Take a look at this," Helen said as she showed Maggie the mug shot of Phillips. Maggie said she had never seen him before.

Helen thanked her and congratulated her on her good fortune. She walked back to her car, and after putting the mug shot back in her briefcase, she started the engine and drove back to her office. On the way back, she remembered she had forgotten that the FBI could, sometimes, restore ground-off serial numbers on guns. So, as soon as she arrived back at her office, she had the gun used to kill Ben Barlow sent to the FBI to see if they could bring back the ground-off numbers.

CHAPTER NINETEEN

Ken Matthews left on the early flight the following morning. After checking into the hotel where a reservation had been made for him, he went directly to the Walla Walla Police Department. Detective Brett Sampson, the detective he had spoken to on the telephone the day before, was waiting for him. Detective Sampson had pulled the file on the Mary Phillip's murder case and had it ready for Ken to review. From this file, he learned Mary Phillips had been shot as she was walking on the sidewalk about a block from her house at about 9:00 a.m. There had been no witnesses, and interviews with her friends disclose no information of value.

Ralph Phillips was immediately suspected of this crime, mainly because his wife had taken out a life insurance policy on herself about six months earlier. The policy was for $200,000, and Ralph Phillips was the beneficiary. Phillips admitted he knew about the insurance policy but denied having anything to do with his wife's death. He claimed he had worked until almost midnight the night before at the sports bar where he was employed. He claimed he had gone to bed about an hour after he got home that morning and was still asleep when the police woke him to tell him about his wife's death. He said she always took a walk after she ate breakfast every morning.

The sports bar's employment records verified Phillips's claim. The other employees, when interviewed, said Phillips had not been away from his job at any time during his employment period.

From the file, Ken got a list of all acquaintances who were interviewed during the investigation. None of them had any reason to suspect Phillips, and the case was still unsolved. It was still active, but no leads had come up in several months. There was a notation that since Mary's first husband had been murdered too, Ralph Phillips was a suspect in that murder also. A review of that file turned up no information of value.

Since Ralph Phillips had not been tried for any crime, the insurance company paid the $200,000 to him. The next day, when one of the detectives went to his house, he was not there. They checked at his place of employment, and he had not reported in for work. He has never been seen again.

There was a notation in the file that about three years before, Phillips had another wife who was shot and killed in Portland, Maine. There was another notation that the night before Mary was murdered, there was a break-in at a nearby house, and among the things taken was a .38-caliber Colt Police Special revolver. It was a gun owned by the grandson of a retired FBI agent who had inherited it when his grandfather died. There was another notation that read that since his wife's husband had been murdered earlier, consider Ralph Phillips a suspect.

When Ken was through reviewing the file, he asked Detective Sampson, "Do you mind if I talk to some of the people that were interviewed during your investigation?"

"No, I don't mind. The case is still unsolved, so maybe you can come up with some new information that will help us solve it."

Ken decided to drive out to the location where the murder occurred. When he got there, the first thing he noticed was the heavy traffic on the street were Mary Phillips was killed. Since he was already out there, he decided to interview persons living on each side of the house where the Phillips had lived. He was lucky. The women who lived in each house was home, and each remembered the murder very well. Both furnished substantially the same information Ken had read in the file, and both pointed out that Phillips could have left his house the morning of the murder and returned without their having seen him, pointing out the rather tall hedge between Phillips's house and their houses. Neither had a picture of Ralph Phillips, but each gave a detailed description of him. Both said Phillips and his wife seemed like nice people, were very friendly, and seemed very much in love.

When he was through talking to each of these women, Ken drove over to an address on Market Street that had been shown as the home of Mary Phillips's best friend. Her name was shown as May Brooks.

When Ken arrived at the address he was seeking, he parked his car in the driveway, walked up to the porch, and rang the doorbell. When he asked to speak to Ms. Brooks, he was told that she had moved about a year and a half ago, and the woman he was talking to did not know where she lived. She added that her next-door neighbor, Janet Saunder's, probably knew where she was now living, but she would not be at home now. She said she worked a split shift at a steak house and usually came home about two o'clock in the afternoon for a couple of hours, so if Ken wanted to see her, he would have to come back then. Otherwise, it would be after 10:00 p.m. before she would be home. She also said she didn't believe the people living on the other side of her house would know Mary because they had only moved in six months ago.

Since it was around noon when Ken finished talking to May Brooks's neighbor, he drove over to a restaurant he had seen a few blocks away as he was driving over to her house. Because she wouldn't be home for a couple of hours, he had plenty of time to get some lunch and return to her house after she came home. After his leisurely lunch, Ken had returned to Janet Saunders house and when he rang the doorbell, she opened the door.

Ken introduced himself and made it clear to her that he was not with the local police department but was from Piedmont, North Carolina, where there had been a murder, and he was trying to locate Ralph Phillips as a person of interest. She immediately told him she had told the local police everything she knew about him three years ago. She added that she had never heard of Piedmont, North Carolina, and certainly had no knowledge as to whether Ralph Phillips was there or not.

Then Ken asked her if she had a photograph of Ralph Phillips. She thought for a moment before saying she thought she might have one. Without saying another word, she turned and walked away, disappearing into the back of the house. She returned, within minutes, with a very good picture of Ralph Phillips standing in front of his house with his wife. "You can keep this," she said as she handed it to him. "Maybe it will help you find him."

After she handed Ken the photograph, she said, "I have trouble believing Ralph killed his wife and is now suspected of killing someone else. He was a quiet and gentle man. He seemed to dote on Mary. I'm aware that people are not always what they seem to be. I hope this picture helps you find him so he can either clear himself or face what he has done."

"Thank you very much, Ms. Saunders. I know how much it hurts when someone betrays you." After Ken finished talking to Janet Saunders, he decided that nothing would be gained by talking to anyone else. The Walla Walla police detectives seemed to have done a good job, and he had the photograph he had come here to find.

After making his decision, he texted Helen and told her what he had accomplished and that he was going to the air terminal to await his plane's departure time.

After Helen agreed with his decision, Ken returned his rental car, returned to the terminal, awaited his departure time, and had a pleasant trip home.

CHAPTER TWENTY

The morning conference started at eight o'clock as always. Since neither Helen Martin nor John Patton had done any work on the case the day before, they had nothing to contribute. Ken Matthews had spent a good portion of last night on a plane coming back from Walla Walla, Washington, but he managed to make it to the meeting on time.

Ken brought them up to date on the murder investigation that occurred in Walla Walla, Washington, about three years earlier and showed them the picture taken of Ralph Phillips with his wife. He told them that he had come up with no new information of value from the persons he talked to. He said the Walla Walla police detectives had done a thorough job but could not get enough information to charge Ralph Phillips with the murder of his wife, and since he was not charged, the insurance company had to pay him the benefits. He said he also attempted to talk to the man who had his Colt Police Special stolen the night before the murder, but he was not available. He was the grandson of a retired and deceased FBI special agent, and the gun meant a lot to him.

While Ken was talking, Helen Martin walked over to the coffeemaker, got herself a cup of black coffee, and sipped on it while listening to his report. When he finished, she walked back to her desk and sat down.

"I'll make copies of the photo and show it to the bowlers and employees at the bowling alley, those who saw the unknown man follow Ben Barlow out the door when he was ordered out by Jesse Moore," she said. "Both of you can work on your other cases, and I'll let you know if anything turns up."

As soon as the meeting was over, Helen made copies of the photograph and took three or four copies with her. She had no sooner gotten into her car and started the engine when she got a call from the dispatcher saying that someone was in the Lambert house and asking for instructions.

"Send two patrol cars over immediately and instruct them to not let the intruder get away. Warn the officers that if the intruder is Ralph Phillips, a white male, about six feet tall, one hundred eight to two hundred pounds, he probably will be armed and dangerous. Tell them that I am on my way and should be there within ten minutes."

Helen immediately turned on the siren and emergency lights and drove as fast as she safely could. When she arrived, Pat Hopkins was standing on her porch and came running to her as she stepped out of the car.

"I have not seen the person in the house," she said, "but when I was walking the dog, I looked over that way, and I could see someone walking around in the house. Then while I was watching, he walked toward the back of the house and disappeared from my view, but he has not come out. My husband was watching the back door, and I was watching the front door until the police officers got here. I called you as soon as I could."

"You did the right thing, Pat," Helen said as Pat's husband came from the back and joined them. "Now, both of you, back into the house, and let us do our job. Please stay in the house until I motion for you to come out."

Helen turned to the patrolman whom she knew. "Come on, Jack, let's ring the doorbell and see what happens."

When they got to the door, Helen rang the doorbell. Both stepped to the side with their guns drawn. They could hear someone coming. The door was opened by a well-dressed man holding some clothes in his arms. He was not carrying a gun in his hand.

"Who are you, and what are you doing here?" Helen demanded.

"I live here," he replied, and then said, "Oh hell, I forgot to notify the police I was coming home." Helen lowered her gun but kept it in her hand. She motioned toward the house next door, where she knew Pat was watching, and beckoned her over.

As soon as Pat started down her porch steps, she saw who the man was. She rushed over and threw her arms around his neck. "Charles Lambert, I thought you were a burglar."

Helen put away her gun and apologized for holding him at gunpoint.

"That's my fault. I should've called you, but I'm glad to know you were on the job. I just came back to pick up a few things and leave without anyone seeing me. I should tell you that I am armed. I have a permit to carry a concealed weapon, but if you want me to, I will hand it to you and let you keep it while I go back into the house and get the things I came for." He showed her the permit, which she examined and handed back to him

"I'm real glad you were not carrying it when you came to the door," Helen said. Then she added, "Now that we have that taken care of, how is your family doing?"

"They are all right. It's only been a few days. How is the investigation coming along?"

"Wait a minute," Helen said. Then she turned to Jack. "You guys can leave. Thanks for the help."

"Glad we could do it. And glad everything turned out okay."

"Me too."

Jack walked toward the back and yelled to the other officer. "Come on, we're through here. Tell you about it over lunch."

"Now," Helen said, "we haven't located him. We are trying as hard as we can, and we will certainly keep you informed when we locate him and have him locked up."

"Well, that's all we can ask for. Now, I have to be going. Sorry I caused so much trouble," Charles said as he started back into the house.

"Wait a minute," Helen called to him. "I have a photo in the car I want you to look at. Wait here and I'll be right back."

Helen ran to the car, grabbed the photograph, and returned with it.

"Take a look at this picture," she said to both Charles and Pat. "Have either of you ever seen either of them before?"

After viewing the photo for a few seconds, both said they had never seen them before. Pat recognized him as the same person whose mug shot Helen had previously shown her.

"Thanks again for watching the house," Charles said to Pat as he turned and started to go back into the house for the second time. This time, he did not return.

Helen turned to Pat. "Thanks for calling."

"I'm sorry I didn't call you personally, but I didn't have your number handy, so I called 911. If I had seen him, or his car, I would have just called and told you Charles was here."

"You did the right thing, Pat."

Just then, Charles backed out of his garage, and they waved goodbye to him. Helen got into her car, waved goodbye to Pat, and started toward the bowling alley. She was disappointed, of course, but she was a seasoned investigator and knew things often do not turn out the way you would like for them to.

When she was about halfway to the bowling alley, Helen passed a Hardee's. As soon as she passed the fast-food restaurant, she had an urge to have a cheeseburger, so she turned the car around and went inside. She ordered a large cheeseburger with tomato and lettuce. She ate it slowly and enjoyed every bite. She followed it with a cold soda, which she seldom drank, and enjoyed every ounce of it also.

After she finished eating, she proceeded on to the bowling alley. As soon as she entered the bowling alley, she walked up to the counter, where Jesse was standing along with his employees and Loretta Jefferson. After the usual pleasantries were exchanged, she showed them the photo of Ralph Phillips with his wife. Each one said they had never seen either.

After they viewed the photograph, Helen ask Loretta if she could remember which of the bowlers said they remembered seeing a man follow Ben Barlow out the bowling alley door on the day he was banished. Loretta said she could and pointed their names out to her. Helen then asked her if she would call each of them and see if they could come to the bowling alley to look at the same photo. "Since they are retired," she said, "hopefully they will all be at home and able to come in."

Helen was lucky. They were home, and each said they would come to the bowling alley as quickly as they could. Jesse yelled over to her as she was calling, telling her he would give them a free game for coming in.

The very first person Helen showed the photo to let out a shriek. "That's my neighbor," she yelled.

"Where does he live?"

"At 2324 Clyde Street."

"How long has he lived there?"

"Well, he was living there when we moved next door to him, twelve years ago." Then she added that he was a sergeant on the police force, and his name was Jacob Blythe.

Helen's hopes were shattered for the second time in the same day. She knew Jacob Blythe, and of course, he was not the killer. The resemblance was remarkable. She wondered why she had not noticed it herself. As the other bowlers came into the bowling alley, Helen showed them the photo, and, as she had expected to happen, each denied knowing the persons in the photograph. She thanked each of them for taking their time to come in and told them to enjoy their free game.

After thanking Jesse Moore and Loretta Jefferson for their assistance, Helen placed a call to Maggie. She wasn't sure whether she was glad or not when Maggie did not answer the telephone because she was tired. She would call her later and arrange to see her in the morning after their eight o'clock conference.

CHAPTER TWENTY-ONE

For the first time since this investigation started, Helen Martin was late for their usual eight o'clock conference. She had, however, texted Ken Matthews, letting him know that she would be late, so he and John Patton poured themselves a cup of coffee and talked about the cases they had worked on the day before. They had each worn a dark suit without a tie. Since they were sitting in Helen's office, they had slipped the jacket off. They had just poured their second cup of coffee when Helen came in. She was neatly dressed in a navy pantsuit with a pale blue blouse.

The first thing she did after she laid her purse and briefcase on her desk was to walk over to the coffee machine and brewed a cup of black coffee. Then she walked back over to her desk and sat down.

"I tried to phone Maggie last night, but she apparently was out late. So I called her again this morning just before I was ready to leave for work, and when she answered, she wanted to talk. We had just finished our conversation when I texted you the message that I would be late," she explained.

"Boy, what a day I had yesterday. Right after I left the office to show the photo you brought back with you yesterday, Ken, I got a call that there was somebody in the Lambert house. I asked the dispatcher to send two officers over to the house to watch the back and front door and not let anybody leave until I could get there.

"As soon as I arrived, I was met by Pat Hopkins who told me there was someone in the house, but she did not know who he was. Jack, a patrolman know, went with me to the front door. We rang the doorbell, and the person who came out was Charles Lambert, the owner. I don't know who was more surprised, him or us."

"Didn't he know the house was being watched?" John asked.

"He said he thought he could just slip into the house, pick up some clothes he needed, and leave quietly without disturbing anyone. He said he appreciated the fact that his house was being watched, and he certainly would not enter it again without notifying us. I showed the Phillipses' photo to him and Pat, and they said they did not recognize either of them.

"Pat and I chatted for a couple of minutes until we saw Charles back out of the garage, and we waved goodbye to him. I thanked Pat for keeping an eye on the place.

"I grabbed a sandwich on the way to the bowling alley. When I got there, I showed the Phillipses' photo to Jesse

Moore and his employees. Each one said they had never seen either of them before. I had the bowlers who had told us they had seen a man follow Ben Barlow as he left the bowling alley on the day he was asked to leave. We had a little excitement at first when one of them said she recognized Phillips. But as it turned out, the person she was talking about was a sergeant on our police force whom I know. My spirits immediately hit the floor."

"Well, I'll have to admit, you had quite a day," Ken said.

"You guys can continue working on your other cases, and I'm going to take the photo and show Maggie to see if she can identify either one of them."

As soon as the conference was over, Helen walked down to her car, started the engine, and drove over to Maggie's. When she drove into the driveway, Maggie was waiting for her. She walked out to the car to greet her.

"I'm really glad to see you, Helen," she said. "I'm sorry I was out last night, but a lady I've become friendly with and I went out to dinner. But now that you're here, come on in, and I will get you a cup of coffee."

"Coffee sounds good, Maggie," Helen said as she walked with her into the house and sat on the sofa. Within minutes, Maggie brought her a steaming cup of black coffee and set it on the coffee table in front of her. Then Maggie started to bring her a tray with sugar and cream. Helen waved her away by telling her she preferred to drink it black.

As she waited for the coffee to cool, Helen handed Maggie the photo of Ralph Phillips and his wife. She looked at the photo for several seconds before saying, "I have never seen either of them before. Have you gotten any more information on them than you had the last time we talked?"

"Yes, I have. We have learned Ralph Phillips is extremely dangerous. What it is believed he has done is kill the husband of a woman, either at random or someone he has chosen for whatever reason. Then he'll wait a few months before he stops by to see the widow and claims he was in town and was going through some old newspapers when he learned an old friend of his, her husband, had been killed few months earlier. He would then tell her he knew him when they were in high school or somewhere, but they had lost touch over the years.

"After they talked awhile, Phillips would express surprise that it was dinner time and invite the widow to eat with him. Acquaintances said he was very personable and was capable of making the woman he was with feel like he was someone she had known for a long time and was someone she liked and trusted. From that time on, they will date for a short time before he proposes, she accepts, and they get married. After a few months, he convinces her to take out a life insurance policy on herself, telling her that if anything would happen to her, he would like to have some extra money to spend on her sons and daughters to help them get over the shock of losing their mother.

"All of what I have told you comes from the people detectives have interviewed during the investigations of two murdered wives of Ralph Phillips."

"He must really be a smooth bastard," Maggie said. "If he comes here, I think I can handle him without any problem. Even if I dated him, I will be in no danger unless I take out an insurance policy on myself. Fat chance that will happen."

"You're probably right, Maggie, but if he comes here, you let me know as soon as he leaves your house. Don't take a chance on calling me while he is here."

"Are there any warrants outstanding for him?"

"No. The detectives could not get enough evidence to charge him with a violation of law. In each case, he used his true name and actually told them he had been in prison because he was in a bar fight and accidentally killed the man who was trying to kill him. He explained that it was self-defense, but the deceased had many friends who testified that he, Phillips, started the fight and killed the other guy for no reason. He was convicted and given a long prison sentence. He said he learned his lesson and has not been in a bar since that time."

"If he comes here, Helen, what good will it do to call you? You have nothing to arrest him for."

"That certainly is a problem, Maggie, but if he shows up, call us and we'll work out something. We certainly do not want you to be hurt."

"Okay, Helen, I'll let you know if he shows up."

"By the way, Maggie, have you thought about how you're going to handle your inheritance after you get the money? You know I told you that I'll be glad to help you decide how to handle it, if you want me to."

"Helen, I thought about it, and I still think I will follow my plans. I'll get the cash, put it in a safe deposit box, and it will be available any time I want it."

"That's not entirely true, Maggie. Your money won't be available unless the bank is open."

"Oh, I thought of that. I'll just keep a few hundred here in a little safe I have, so there won't be any problem."

"All right then, unless you have thought of something that I need to know, that's about all we can do today, but you have my number. Just remember, if Philips shows up, you're dealing with a mass murderer."

"I realize that, Helen, but like I said, I believe I can handle the situation."

"Fine. Keep in touch."

Helen returned to her office.

CHAPTER TWENTY-TWO

Three months passed. No new leads were developed. Maggie had not been contacted by Ralph Phillips, and his whereabouts were still unknown.

The FBI had been able to restore the serial numbers on the gun used in the murder of Ben Barlow. It was the gun that had been stolen in Walla Walla, Washington, from the grandson of a retired and deceased special agent of the FBI.

As soon as she received the information about the gun's owner, Helen contacted him and assured him the gun would be returned to him when it was no longer needed in any legal proceedings.

Helen had gotten to the office early. She was mad. She left word for both Ken Matthews and John Patton to come to her office as soon as they arrived. Both of them arrived a few minutes before 8:00 a.m. and went directly to Helen's office.

As soon as they walked into the office, Helen practically yelled at them. "What kind of detectives are we anyway?"

She picked up her coffee cup, took a sip, and set it down rather hard. She said nothing for a short time. She wanted that question to sink in before continuing.

"It's been overs three months since Ben Barlow was killed. We have identified the person who is probably responsible for his murder and who also sent threatening letters to Jesse Moore and his daughter Jean Lambert. But we have absolutely no idea where he is, or what he intends to do next. What can we do to flush them out?"

John spoke up. "If he follows his usual pattern, he will contact Maggie. When he does, we can arrange to have her meet with him, and we can be there when he shows up. The problem is, although we can hold him for a short time, we have nothing major to charge him with."

"I thought of that," Helen retorted. "But it's been three months, and he has not contacted Maggie. Are we just going to sit here and do nothing?"

Ken answered, "We could run his photo on TV and ask anyone who knows him or who has seen him to call us. The problem is, if we do that and he sees it, he will run."

"At least we will keep Maggie safe," Helen replied.

"Yes, but then he will go on to his next victim after he runs out of the money he got from the insurance companies," Ken said.

John thought for a moment. "He's always used his true name. I don't believe we have contacted our usual sources to see if any of them have a record of a Ralph Phillips."

"How did we let that slip by us?" Helen shouted. "You two get on it now. Let me know immediately what you find out."

Neither John nor Ken had ever seen Helen this riled up before. They divided the list of their sources, left the building, and were back before lunch. As soon as they were back, they contacted Helen and returned to her office.

"What did you find out?" she inquired.

They both had to tell her that their sources had no record of Ralph Phillips.

She stood up behind her desk. "This is what I'm going to do," she said. "I'll give Phillips two more weeks to contact Maggie. If he doesn't, I'll give his picture to all the media sources. Sorry I yelled at you, but we can't just keep sitting on our hands doing nothing. So like I said, we will wait two more weeks before asking the media for help."

Eleven days passed, and then just as Helen was leaving the office around six o'clock that evening, her telephone rang. "He's been here," Maggie said excitedly. "Come over, and I'll tell you all about it."

"Great!" Helen exclaimed. "I'll be there as quick as possible. I assume he's not still there."

"No, he left, but he's coming back in a couple of days. I'll give you the whole story when you get here."

Helen grabbed her briefcase and ran to her car. Just as she was about to get into the car, she saw Ken walking toward his car. She called over to him, "We've got a break, Ken. Hop in and go with me."

As soon as Ken was in the car, Helen told him what happened. He became as excited as she was and anxiously awaited their meeting with Maggie. Within fifteen minutes, they were at her residence. As soon as they parked the car and started toward her front door, Maggie opened the door and motioned for them to step inside.

"Okay, Maggie," Helen said without any greetings, "tell us everything that happened."

"At two thirty, my doorbell rang. I answered it, and there stood Ralph Phillips. I recognized him from his photograph, but of course, I acted like I didn't know who he was. He gave me his name and told me he had come into town on business. He said that when he was going through some old newspapers that had been stacked up in his room, he noticed an old friend of his had been shot and killed in the bowling alley. He said as he read more, he saw my name and address and had come over to express his sorrow. Then he asked me if he could come in."

When Maggie paused, Ken said, "Then what happened?"

"He gently put his arm around my shoulders and quietly said, 'My wife died a few months ago, so I know what you are going through.' He said I had to go on living, but at times it would be terribly hard. I agreed with him that it was very hard to keep going, but I was doing my best.

"When I asked him where he had known my husband, he said, 'I'm ashamed to tell you this. I met him when we were in prison together.' Frankly, Helen, I don't know if my husband had ever been in prison or not, but I didn't question him. Then he glanced at his watch. It was a couple of minutes after four. He told me he usually ate early and asked me if I would join him at a restaurant of my choice. Of course, I said yes. After all, I was getting a free meal."

Maggie paused. She excused herself, went to the kitchen, got a drink of water, and returned.

She continued. "We walked down the street to Sandy's, where we had a drink and a nice early dinner. During our meal, we talked about nothing important. He is a very smooth conversationalist.

"When we were through eating, we walked back to my apartment. He walked me to the door, gave me a hug, and said that he felt like he had known me for months and would like to see me again. I said, 'You know, it's strange, but I feel the same way.' I told him I hadn't been out with anyone except him since my husband died, and I didn't know if I could be good company or not, but I would like to try. I said there was a movie on that I hadn't seen, and I would enjoy seeing it with him. At that point, he said he had been offered a transfer to Piedmont, and now that he had met me, he thought he would accept it. We have a date in two nights."

"I don't know about that," Helen said. "You know what has happened to his two wives."

"Yes, I know. But he is not going to harm me unless we get much better acquainted and he can figure out a way get my money."

"Well, we don't have to worry about that anyway, since we will be here to pick him up when he calls on you."

"Why?" Maggie said. "I've been thinking about this, Helen. What good is it going to do if you pick him up when you have nothing to charge him with? I know you can hold him for a short time, but this guy is not going to admit anything. Based on the short time I spent with him, I can tell you that."

"Then what are we going to do, Maggie? We can't just pretend he's not here and take no action."

"I know this type of guy, Helen. He has a very high ego, and I can use that ego. I've thought of a plan. Give me a month, and I think I will have an admission from him. I want you to bug my apartment, and I'll give you a room where you can hear everything that is said. I really believe that in one month's time, I can get him to admit that he killed my husband."

"That, Maggie, would be against everything I have ever learned."

"What have you got to lose, Helen?"

"My job, Ken's Job, John's job, and if things don't go right, another dead body named Maggie."

"He's not going to hurt me, Helen, unless he gets to the point of asking me to marry him, I accept, and within a short time, I take out an insurance policy making him the beneficiary. That is not going to happen. He doesn't care whether I live or die, except to get my money. As soon as you hear him make his confession, you'll be there with your other detectives, and he will be all yours. Like I said, what have you got to lose? Right now you have nothing, and you know he is not going to confess if you pick him up and question him. All that will do is cause him to run and open up somewhere else. I know men, or at least men like him. If I fail, then you will be there to pick him up, but if you and the other detectives stay away from him, I sincerely believe I can get him to confess to me."

"What are you going to do exactly, Maggie?"

"I'm going to get very friendly. I'll hate every minute of it, but I can do it. I want that bastard in jail for the rest of his life. Give me a chance. If this works out, and I fully believe it will, then I'll tell you the story of my life. But don't try tailing him or do any more investigation, or he could get wind of it and vanish. Let me have my chance."

"Maggie, you make a good argument. For some crazy reason, I think you can do it. One month, and we pull the plug." Helen looked at Ken. "What do you think, Ken?"

"I think it's our only chance to get this guy off the streets. I'm like you. For some reason, I believe she can do it."

"Okay. Have your lab guys come over tomorrow. You come with them. I'll show you where you can stay, and they can see where the bugs need to go. I will only need to have the bedroom bugged. I do not want to know where they are placed. Can you come around two o'clock?"

"I'll have to ask the lab guys, but I'll let you know if they can't make it."

When they were back in the car, Helen said, "Have we lost our minds?"

"Yes," Ken acknowledged.

CHAPTER
TWENTY-THREE

As soon as John Patton reported for work, he checked his voice mail. He had gotten a notice from Helen Martin requesting him to come to her office at eight o'clock to meet with her and Ken Matthews. Since he had come in a few minutes early, he checked the rest of his messages but found nothing that had to be worked on immediately.

As soon as he saw Helen, he knew something was up. She was dressed in a neat green business suit with a light yellow blouse. She had a different look about her than she had the last few days. She looked like she was extremely pleased about something.

"Well," he said, "are we celebrating St. Patrick's Day early?"

"No, but we are celebrating. Yesterday, as I was leaving work, I got a call from Maggie. Ralph Phillips had contacted her. As I was getting into the car, I saw Ken coming out, and I motioned for him to join me, and we went over to see her."

"Great. When do we pick him up?"

"In one month."

John obviously looked puzzled.

"Sit down, John, and I'll tell you everything that happened. When Ken and I got to Maggie's, she told us all about Phillips contacting her and everything he had said and done. It followed the same pattern he used when he first met the two women he married and is suspected of killing.

"When I told Maggie we would be there to pick Phillips up when he came to see her the next time, which is supposed to be in two days, she said one word, 'Why?' Then she added, 'What can you charge him with?'

"When I got to thinking, I realize she was right. We can pick him up as a suspect in the murder of Ben Barlow and hold him for a short time, but we have absolutely no evidence to show he killed anybody. Then she told us that if we would give her one month, she would get a confession from him."

"I'm confused as hell," John said. "Did you agree to let Phillips walk the streets for a month?"

"Yes, we did, John. If you had heard her, you would be convinced. He is not going to run unless we spook him. He's not going to hurt her until he can benefit by her death. She laid out a plan to have her house bugged so we can listen to everything that goes on while she is getting him to confess. We are to take our lab guys over there at 2:00 p.m. today if their schedule will permit them to do so. At first glance, her plan makes no sense, but when you think about it, it's about our only chance to get this guy off the streets. All he is after from her is money, and until he has a good chance of getting it, she will be very important to him, and he will treat her well."

"I'm sure you realize, Helen, how much we are sticking our necks out. If this fails, we're all going to be looking for work, and who's going to employ detectives that allowed a fugitive to walk away?"

"That's the problem, John. He's not a fugitive. There are no charges pending against him anywhere. I know we're sticking our necks out, but I really believe she'll do what she says she can. I hope you will agree to go along with Ken and me."

"Have you gotten approval for this, Helen?"

"No, and I'm not going to. For one reason, we could never get it approved. If this works, we will be heroes. If it fails, we will be bums, or worse, and Phillips will walk again, but that's exactly what he will do if we pick him up now."

"Okay, Helen, I've worked with you a long time, and I've learned to trust your instincts. I think we're nuts, but I also realize that we really don't have any other real choice."

"Fine, fine," Helen replied. "It's going to be a long month, but we can do nothing, and I mean nothing at all, about Ralph Phillips. If he gets even a hint that we are involved, he will run. We will work on our other cases until Maggie gets in touch with us."

As soon as the meeting was over, Helen picked up her phone and called Maggie. "It's in your hands, Maggie. Unless I call you back, the lab techs and I will be over to your place at two o'clock. Do you have any doubts about what you're going to be doing?"

"No, I do not. It's going to be the hardest thing I have ever done because Ralph Phillips will think I have fallen madly in love with him, and I will act accordingly. I'll try not to throw up while I'm doing it, but I just can't let that son of a bitch walk away again."

When she hung up on Maggie, Helen called Herman Kimball, chief of the Piedmont Police Department laboratory and asked him if she could come over to see him.

"Sure. Is this a friendly visit, or do you have some work for us?"

"Both. I'll tell you when I get there. Have me a cup of coffee ready."

As soon as Helen walked into the lab, Herman gave her a big hug. "Glad to see you, Helen. Everybody's been so busy lately, we don't get to see much of each other." Then he handed her a cup of hot black coffee.

"Herman, I need something done that must be kept quiet. I'm sticking my neck out by doing what I'm going to ask you to do, but I hope to catch a serial killer, and frankly, I can't think of any other way to do it. I have a residence that needs to be bogged with the occupant's approval, but nothing will happen for one month. I need you to do it personally and, if possible, alone. If our plan fails, I will protect you by having the necessary approval in your hands."

"Man, you sound serious, Helen."

"I am serious, Herman. Without going into all the details, we've got a suspect who has killed at least three men and two women after he got out of prison. He is probably going to try to get insurance money from the occupant of the house by killing her. She is going to work with us. She will have to be an extremely good actress doing a job that she will despise."

"What do you want me to do, Helen? And where do you want me to do it? I know how you brought down that thug George Spuri, and I will trust you to do the same with this guy."

"Okay, Herman, are you free at two o'clock today? If you are, I'll buy you lunch."

"Yeah, I can get away. And I'll take you up on your offer for lunch."

"Good, I knew I could count on you. I'll pick you up at twelve thirty, and we'll go over to Duncan's, if that's all right with you."

"That's fine with me. It's a little fancy, but I can handle it. See you then."

"Thanks, Herman," Helen said as she turned and walked out the door.

* * * * *

After Helen and Herman had a very nice leisurely lunch during which they talked about nothing serious, she took him to Maggie's. As soon as they rang the doorbell, Maggie welcomed them. Helen introduced her to Herman and told her he would be doing the work.

"Fine," she replied. "I think I told you before that I only wanted the bedroom bugged, but I believe, to be safe, we should also bug the kitchen. I don't know what that involves, and I do not want to know where they are placed. So, Herman, when you're ready to do the work, I'll leave the house and not return until you're through."

"Let me get this straight, Maggie. You want every word said in your kitchen and bedroom recorded and listened to by Helen and her fellow detectives."

"That's right. Now if you'll come with me, I'll show you the bedroom. You can see the kitchen from here. I want it set up so that Helen and the other two detectives can hear everything that's said while they are in the other bedroom."

Herman examined the bedroom and assured Maggie it would be no problem. He looked at kitchen over and told her the same thing about it. As soon as he had inspected the bedroom and the kitchen, they all went into the other bedroom, where Herman said he could set up a listing post with no problem at all. He said the whole job would only take about an hour. He said he could do the work by himself. Maggie said she would rather wait a couple of weeks to make sure she still believes what she intends to do will work.

* * * * *

Helen continued to work on her regular cases. Each day seemed like it had forty hours in it while she waited for Maggie's call. When the allotted time neared the end, Helen was a nervous wreck. She forced herself not to call Maggie, but she was beginning to wonder if she had been taken for a fool.

Finally, two days before the time expired, Maggie called Helen and said the time had come to place the equipment in the house. Helen got in touch with Herman, and they went over to Maggie's. Herman went to work. Maggie left the house like she said she would, and Helen watched Herman work. When he finished putting the hidden microphones in, he went into the spare bedroom with Helen and set up the listening post. Then they tested the equipment, and Helen could hear every word said in every part of the bedroom and every part of the kitchen.

After the equipment was tested, Herman gave Helen a course on how to turn it on and how to test it. After that was done, they called Maggie, and she returned home.

After Maggie arrived home, they brought her up to date. Then she told them to come there at 3:00 p.m. the day after tomorrow. Ralph would be there at 5:00 p.m. to pick her up, and she wanted all of them to be in the house before they left because they had a neighborhood watch, and she did not want someone calling the police because they saw three strangers entering her place after she and Ralph left. She also said she would place a cooler in the room with sandwiches in it as well as soft drinks and water. The bedroom had a bathroom in it, so they should be comfortable.

Helen thanked Maggie. She told her that in the unlikely event of equipment failure, she would call Maggie's cell phone and say one word, "Off."

They were ready. The scene was set.

CHAPTER TWENTY-FOUR

At 2:30 p.m., Helen Martin, with Ken Matthews and John Patton, left her office en route to Maggie's apartment. Helen went alone in her car. Ken and John rode together in Ken's car. They took two cars so when the time came to arrest Ralph Phillips, he could be put into the car with Ken and John to be taken to jail, and Helen would have her car to return home.

Although it was only a fifteen-minute drive to Maggie's, they wanted to scout the neighborhood carefully before walking up to her apartment. When they were satisfied no one was watching the apartment, they parked their cars a block away and walked back.

Maggie answered the door as soon as they rang the doorbell and invited them in. Maggie was in the process of making some sandwiches for the three detectives to eat if they got hungry while waiting in the bedroom where the listening post was located. Helen helped her finish preparing the sandwiches. John and Ken put a few soft drinks in the cooler Maggie furnished. They appreciated what she was doing for them because once they entered the room, they would remain there until Maggie called for them to come out. They could not wander around the apartment after Maggie left with Ralph Phillips for fear that someone would see them and call the police.

After everything was in place in the bedroom, Helen activated the recording equipment. She and Maggie entered Maggie's bedroom and carried on a conversation almost in a whisper. Every word they said was heard clearly by Ken and John.

Satisfied that everything was in working order, they socialized until shortly before 5:00 p.m. Maggie had told them Ralph was usually punctual. She said they were going to eat dinner and then go to a movie. She guessed they would be back between ten and eleven o'clock. She reminded them, although they did not need any reminding, to turn off their cell phones before she and Ralph returned.

As soon as the three of them entered the room housing the listening post, they closed and locked the door. They turned off all communication devices. They talked quietly among themselves about nothing of importance until they heard the doorbell ring. Then absolute quiet prevailed.

After Ralph Phillips rang the doorbell, Maggie opened the door and gave him an affectionate greeting. Then she grabbed her purse. She took hold of his arm and started walking him out the door. "I'm sure looking forward to tonight," she said as they walked out the door and got into his car. "Where are you taking me tonight?"

"I'm going to surprise you, but I'll give you a hint. They make the best martinis in town."

Maggie guessed a couple of restaurants, but Ralph said no each time. After she made the second wrong guess, they pulled up in front of the best Italian restaurant in the city. "Oh, I love this place," Maggie said as they got out of the car and turned it over to the valet to park. They entered the restaurant, and since it was an early weeknight, they were quickly seated.

When they were comfortably seated, the waitress took their drink order. In no time at all, she returned with their drinks. After placing their drinks on the table, the waitress did not return until they had almost finished drinking them. While they were drinking, they checked the menu, so they were ready to place their orders as soon as she came to the table.

When the waitress returned with their dinner, they ate with little conversation. After they finished eating, they went to the theater and arrived just fifteen minutes before the movie they wanted to see started. By the time they got their tickets and were seated, the movie was ready to start.

After the movie was over, they drove back to Maggie's, parked the car in the driveway, and walked up to the front door. Maggie rang the doorbell and then got out her key and opened the door.

Ralph watched as Maggie rang the doorbell but said nothing until they were inside. Then he said, "Why did you ring the doorbell? You live here."

Maggie laughed. "Oh, that's just to give the burglars time to get out."

"Now, why didn't I think of that?" he responded.

"I had a great evening, Ralph. I'll show you how much I appreciated it later," she promised.

Ralph answered, "I'm sure going to hold you to that promise."

"I won't forget, but first, would you like another drink? I can make a pretty good martini too."

"I've had enough to drink, and I'm ready to collect on your promise."

Every word they said had been heard and recorded. Then the detectives heard them as they walked across the floor into Maggie's bedroom. A short time later, Ken said, "They are having sex." Although he said this in a whisper, Helen put her finger to her lips.

After a few minutes, the detectives heard what seemed to be Maggie softly sobbing.

"What's the matter, honey?" Ralph asked. "Did I do something?"

"No, you didn't do anything. I'm just sad because I don't know who shot my husband."

"Why did you think of that just now?" Ralph asked. "The police are doing everything they can to catch him."

"I don't want to know who it is to give his name to the police. I want to reward him for getting rid of my husband, who was not always nice to me, and for bringing you into my life. The only other good thing my husband did was leaving me a lot of money, and I'd like to share it with the guy who took him out. I've just never known anybody as nice as you before."

Ralph picked up on her statement that she had been left a lot of money. "What do you mean, he left you a lot of money? Did he have a lot of insurance? I thought he was a fugitive."

"Well, I usually don't talk about money with people I don't know, but somehow I feel like I've known you forever, and I know I can trust you."

"I don't want to pry into your finances unless you want me to, but if you feel like you need to talk to me about something, you know I will do anything I can for you."

"Well, you know, if you read the paper, that he was wanted for bank robbery. I knew he had a safe deposit box with a lot of money in it. I just thought he was a flimflam artist, since he pretended to be a financial advisor. Anyway, the one good thing he did was put my name on the safe deposit box papers so that I am the beneficiary. Now, I've got a lot of money. And if I knew who killed him, I would be more than happy to share it."

"Are you saying that if you knew who he was, you would not turn him in to the police? How much money are you talking about, anyway?"

"No, I wouldn't turn him in. Like I said, I want to give him a reward for bringing you to me. I have about a half million dollars, so I can spare some."

This is going to be easy, Ralph thought, *and I probably won't even have to kill her.* "What if I told you I killed him?"

"Don't be silly, Ralph, I know you wouldn't hurt anybody. You are the kindest man I know. Why would you want to kill him?"

"I had seen you around. I fell in love with you. I saw the way he treated you, so I got rid of him."

"Quit saying that, Ralph. I'm serious."

"So am I, Maggie. I killed him. I should get a reward for helping the FBI close their case."

"Okay, if you insist on saying you did it, what was he killed with?"

"A gun."

"Okay, you've had your fun, Ralph. Everybody in town knows he was killed with a gun. If you had really killed him, you would have told me what kind of gun and what you did with it. Turn over and go to sleep."

"Maggie, do you really want to know who killed Ben, or were you just talking?"

"I really want to know, like I told you."

"Okay. I am serious, Maggie. I killed Ben. I shot him with a Colt snub-nosed revolver, and I threw it on the bowling alley floor." He laughed. "How much do I get as my reward?"

"All you are entitled to." Then she shouted, "He's all yours, Helen!"

All three detectives burst into the room with Helen leading. Ken and John quickly yanked Ralph Phillips out of the bed and handcuffed his hands behind his back.

"What? What is going on?" Phillips yelled. "Give me my pants."

Helen did not wait for John to pull Phillips's pants on him. She said, "You are under arrest for the murder of Ben Barlow." Then she started to read him his Miranda rights.

He stopped her. "I know my rights." Then he turned to Maggie. "You are good," he told her, "but I'll be out in a day or two, and I better not see you."

"You won't be out for a long time, if ever, Ralph," Helen said. "Take him out of here and book him, John." Ken and John slipped Ralph's pants on him. Then they slipped a loop in a previously prepared clothesline over one of his feet before putting his shoes on. Helen put his shirt over his shoulders. Ken and John each took hold of an arm and led him out the door.

"It's been a long month, Maggie. I could not have done what you did."

"Ben was not honest, Helen, but I loved him. He did not deserve to be shot and left on the floor like that."

"No, he didn't, Maggie, but you avenged him," Helen said as she turned to leave.

"I will not forget my promise to you, Helen."

Chapter Twenty-Five

As soon as they closed the door behind them as they left Maggie's apartment, Ralph Phillips said, "Take these cuffs off me so I can put my shirt on."

"The cuffs stay on," Ken told him. "Now, this is what we are going to do. We are going to walk to our car. It's a block away. If you try to get away, I'll pull on this rope, and you will fall flat on your face. Do we understand each other?"

"Yeah, I understand you," Ralph mumbled.

"That's good. Start walking."

Ralph started walking as instructed. He said nothing more and gave them no trouble on the walk to the car. He was put in the backseat of the car on the passenger side with John sitting beside him.

Before Ken could get the car started, Ralph, said, "Wait a minute, before you start the car. How would you like $25,000 apiece? You could take your families on one hell of a vacation," he added without giving either Ken or John a chance to answer him.

"You are not too smart, Ralph. You've just added attempted bribery to your resume. You better keep that money. You are going to need it for your attorney."

Ralph did not respond. He sat there and stayed quiet until they arrived at the jail. They took him in. He was fingerprinted, booked, and led off to his cell. In answer to his question, Ralph was told he would be notified when his hearing would be scheduled. Then after his hearing, he was ordered held without bond.

CHAPTER TWENTY-SIX

Helen Martin returned from the hearing pleased with the way it went. She had a call from Maggie telling her she was ready to talk. She returned the call, and Maggie agreed to come to her office right away.

As soon as Maggie entered her office, Helen said, "Before you sit down, Maggie, are you going to be truthful with me?"

"This time, I will be absolutely truthful, even if I have broken some laws."

"All right," Helen said. "Let's start with you telling me your true name."

"Well, to start with, I was with Ben a few years longer than I told you I was. As I told you before, I was a waitress, and Ben did ask me out. Within a few weeks, I was in love with him. We were married in Las Vegas. We got married under the name of Yelson. I thought that was his real name. Of course, the tale I told you about having a guy with the name of Nick marrying us was all bull, but I thought it was a pretty good story."

"It was a pretty good story, Maggie, and I thought you were awfully dumb to have that happen to you, but I didn't know you well enough then to really question it."

"What I just told you, Helen, is the truth. I know now Yelson is not my name, but I did not know it before. All my papers are in the name of Yelson. My wedding license, my driver's license. Right now I don't know what my marital status is. I don't know if a person can be married under an alias or not."

"That is something you will have to get legal advice on, Maggie. Frankly, I don't know. Anyway, you told me that Ben called himself a financial advisor, but we now know that he robbed banks and probably other places. According to his former partner, he rented a safe deposit box, and there was probably several hundred thousand dollars in that box. Did you know that most of the money, if not all of it, came from armed robberies? Did you know about the safe deposit box?"

"No, I did not know he was an armed robber. For a long time, I didn't know he had a safe deposit box with a lot of cash in it. I did know he always seemed to have money, and we lived well. I suspected he was a flimflam artist because every few months we moved in a hurry. After we had lived together for a couple of years, Ben told me about the box for the first time and made me the beneficiary. He did this by taking me to the bank, and he signed the papers in my presence. You probably suspected that my story about my unknown uncle leaving me a lot of money was a lot of crap. I really don't know why I told you that in the first place."

"Now, I'll tell you a story, Maggie. We've had so much work that we added another detective. When he was going over our cases, as soon as he saw what you said about your unknown uncle leaving you all that money, he said, 'That story about her uncle might explain how she can live without working, but it's as phony as a three-dollar bill.'"

"Helen, what I just told you about the safe deposit box is true. I have been drawing money from it, and it does have a very large amount of cash in it."

"Ben must have been good at what he did," Helen mumbled under her breath. "You know how much cash is in the box now, or where it came from?"

"No. I have not counted it, and I really have no idea where it came from. Do you think it will be taken from me?"

"I don't know, Maggie. That's a decision the DA will have to make. Of course, I will tell him everything you have told me and everything you have done to solve the murder case. You may want to get an attorney. The one you get to determine if you are legally married or not could probably handle this too."

"I have not exactly been a model, have I, Helen?"

"I would say that's a pretty accurate statement," Helen replied. "Is there anything I should know about that you have not told me? I don't like surprises."

"No. That's pretty much my life story. It is the truth. I might add the reason I never reported Ben missing at first was because he did stay out some nights or a couple of days without telling me he was to be away. That was another thing that caused me to think that perhaps his activities were not entirely legal."

"Tell me, Maggie, did you just think Ben's activities were illegal, or did you know they were not?"

"Did I have proof his activities were not legal? No. Did he tell me his activities were not legal? No, but I couldn't help but wonder because of the way we lived."

"Is there anything else you need to tell me about? That I did not ask you?"

"No. I have told you everything that I can think of."

Helen stood up. "Maggie, you are an interesting person. I hope the rest of your life can be spent with friends, and hopefully, in time, you will meet an honest man you can grow old with."

"You know, Helen, I believe I will." With that said, Maggie turned and walked out the door.

EPILOGUE

Ralph Phillips was tried and convicted for the murder of Ben Barlow. He was sentenced to life in prison without parole. He appealed. The sentence was upheld.

During his fifth year in prison, Ralph found God because of the influence of the prison ministry. After that, he confessed to the murders in Portland, Maine, and Walla Walla, Washington. He also admitted to writing the threatening letters to Jesse Moore and his daughter, Jean Lambert. He lived the remainder of his life in prison.

Maggie was able to keep the money in the safe deposit box because it could not be determined where the money came from. She became interested in helping the homeless. While volunteering, she met and married a respectable businessman.

Jean and Charles Lambert sold their house and stayed in Ohio near his brother. Bobbi goes to make many flights with her uncle in his airplane.

Helen Martin, Ken Matthews, and John Patton were recognized for the great work they did in the investigation of the murder of the man left on the floor of the bowling alley.

Printed in the United States
By Bookmasters